ZOMBIE ZERO
THE LAST ZOMBIE

ZOMBIE ZERO
THE LAST ZOMBIE

J.K. NORRY

Zombie Zero: The Last Zombie

Copyright © 2016 by J.K. Norry
Cover Art: Sean Harrington

Publishers note:
This book is a work of fiction. Names, characters, places and incidents are either the product of the author's imagination or are used fictitiously, and any resemblance to actual persons living or dead, events, or locales is entirely coincidental.

All rights reserved. No part of this book may be reproduced in any form by any electronic or mechanical means including photocopying, recording, or information storage and retrieval without permission in writing from the author.

ISBN-13: 978-1-944916-80-0

www.SuddenInsightPublishing.com
Indie publishing for the Indie Author

Acknowledgements

This project was a way for me to say many things, while telling a sometimes fun and sometimes gruesome story about zombies. One of the things I was trying very hard to say with this book was 'thank you'. My life has been inspired and guided by enough people that it would take an entire book to list them. But some folks are special, and stand out as special in the way they inspire me. I included many of them in this book, and the first volume, in a way that was designed to pay homage and show deep respect. Although I do not claim that the representations of these people in the books stand for them in any way in real life, I do sincerely hope that everyone that was included is pleased with how this fictitious version of them handled things.

I would like to take this opportunity to thank everyone who made it possible for these books to take this form.

Doctor Christopher Ryan was in the prologue to 'Zombie Zero: The First Zombie'. His character didn't make it past the prologue, but don't take that to mean I am not a great admirer of this man's brilliant work. Read 'Sex at Dawn' for an honest and informative look at the history of human sexuality, and ask yourself if you really want a 'traditional' relationship when you are through. Thank you, Doctor Ryan.

Ari Shaffir has a podcast called 'The Skeptic Tank'. If you like your humor dark and dry and smart, you might want to take things to the next level like Ari has and go see him perform. You'll definitely want to check out his podcast. I've never missed an episode. Thanks, Ari!

Adam Dreece is someone I've been watching closely for awhile. First I admired him from afar, and put him on my 'True Professionals' list; then I starting reading his books, and was delighted by the warm creativity and welcoming imagination of this engaging storyteller. There's a reason he is one of the first real-life mentions in the '*Zombie Zero: The First Zombie*', and why he plays such a big role. Thanks, Adam!

Christina Hoff Sommers explores the deeper meaning of feminism with startling insight. She single-handedly battles 'The War Against Boys' and asks the question 'Who Stole Feminism' with her incredible books and video blog, 'The Factual Feminist'. She also shows how philosophy is relevant to society, and how philosophers can help shape it, by setting high standards in research and insight for the social commentator. Wow, that's a lot to be thankful for. Thanks, Christina!

Christina McMullen is an author that I discovered online not long ago. As soon as I read one of her books, I knew I had to read them all. It wasn't just that I loved the way her mind worked; I deeply admired the way she translated it into her screamingly entertaining stories. As with my other favorite authors, I read her books as both an appreciative audience and a student of greatness. You can't imagine how delighted I was to get to include her in all of this. Thanks, Christina!

Megan O'Russell takes both her passion and her professionalism very seriously. I knew that I loved her writing, then I discovered that she is quite dedicated to acting as well. With her giving spirit and her considerable talent, I felt safe putting her in a bit of a predicament in the first book. Don't worry, fans of her writing and acting will get to find out where she ends up in the pages to follow. Thanks, Megan!

Rolawndo Swells is actually a good friend of mine. He read a couple of my books, and sent me an email. We live close to each other, and he bought the books at a winery, so he proposed that we share a glass or two some time. Soon we graduated to visiting each other at home, and to drinking whisky while talking about all sorts of things. One of those things is his upcoming novel, which he is putting serious and passionate work into getting finished. Now, I look forward to reading his books too! Thanks, Rolawndo!

Angela B. Chrysler has been influencing and helping me since I first stepped into the world of the indie author. From championing other peoples' books to writing her own, Angela takes special care crafting the perfect vehicle for the occasion. She takes writing in multiple genres to places only she could go, and shows herself to be as multi-faceted and fascinating as the books she writes by writing them. If you want more of me after reading all my books, or without having to, I'm about as honored as I can be to have been brought aboard as a character in her blog series 'Zombies From Space…And Vampires!'. You might check that out, along with her many other ambitious and impressive endeavors. Thanks, Captain! (Read her series; you'll get it.)

Doug Benson is not just a hilarious comic and great movie reviewer; he's also a bit of a podcast king. I saw his movies and comedy specials, and then got hooked on his show. Some folks don't expect much from a guy who has a movie called 'Super High Me' or a podcast called 'Getting High With Doug', but most of us know the truth by now: those folks are the real dopes. Doug is a true professional, and he is easy to admire in both his artistic ability and his business sense. Thanks, Doug!

Sarah Barthel and Josh Carter are the sonic phenomenon that is Phantogram. Their music is some next level stuff, and it stirs my soul to listen to it. These two worked incredibly hard to make sure the world learned how incredible they are together, and it is a testament to their great talent and their hard work that just about everyone has fallen for their sublime sounds by now. And Leroy, Sarah's adorable little dog…we've all fallen for him as well. Thanks, Sarah, Josh and Leroy!

Michael R. Stern and his wife Linda are both authors. She writes as L.C. Bennett Stern, and is the author of 'Bosses and Blackjacks'. Michael has turned what began as a fun adventure into a true time-traveling legacy. With his love and knowledge of history, he makes time travel come alive like no one else; and with a keen eye for dark details, he peels back the layers of a story with a special skill. Thanks, Michael and Linda!

Joe Compton wrote 'Amongst the Killing', and got an offer from a traditional publisher for it. He did a little math, and met some folks in the indie author community, and decided to join their ranks instead. By the time I joined those ranks, he had already helped countless other independent authors with their books. With 'Go Indie Now', Joe has helped transform what was already a friendly and welcoming community to a hugely helpful and supportive one as well. Thanks, Joe!

Tom Corson Knowles is someone else that I discovered through my love of podcasts. He's one of those people that many folks think were born lucky, as everything he touches seems to turn to gold. The rest of us know that it took monumental hard work for him to get where he is. Now Tom makes it a habit to touch the lives of others, and help us walk the path he worked so hard to forge with him. Anyone in the writing or publishing world can benefit from listening to the 'Publishing Profits Podcast' every week. I know I do. Thanks, Tom!

T. Harv Eker was one of the first people to really impress the importance of a well-rounded and happy life upon me. He did so through his brilliant and insightful book, 'Secrets of the Millionaire Mind', one of the many avenues through which he has helped countless people. Without proclaiming himself so, Harv is a great example of a relevant modern philosopher. Rather than sit back and comment on the world, he has learned to live in it and love it for all it has to offer. Thanks, Harv!

These books could not be taking shape as they are without my partner in all things, Dawn Marshall. I would like to sincerely thank her for working so hard every day to make my dream come true, and for giving life to my legacy. Our partnership is the platform from which I launch everything these days, and I have her to thank for the solid foundation she has built while I have had my face stuck in a laptop. Thanks, Dawn!

There are two very special beings that have touched my life and my heart in ways that I had never imagined. They can't read this, or at least they pretend not to be able to; but I've got to say it anyway. Mammoth was Dawn's dog until we got together. It didn't take long before he became my good buddy, and 'our dog' instead. I sensed he might be a bit lonely, and that led us to the SPCA. There we found a small adorable angel who soon became much more than a little sister to my good buddy. Thanks to Mammoth and Ximena, for all the love and friendship.

It's an awkward thing for me to talk about, although I take great liberty in writing about it; but it's important to note that I am a big fan of God in the form it which it makes sense to me, and a great admirer of Mother Earth. I can't feel that something like this could have ever been started or finished without some feeling of connection to these things as I write and live. So…thanks God, for everything. And big thanks to Mother Earth, for playing such a big role in these books and my life.

Another very special part of becoming an author and taking that role seriously has become part of my life these last few years. I always felt especially connected to my favorite authors, and used to wonder how that felt from the other side of the page. Writers seemed to live in another world to me then, a world untouched by common influences and opinions.

It took learning and experience to show me what I should have known all along. There are endless reasons to write, an unlimited number of stories to be told, and boundless rewards to be found in courting the muse. But there is only one reason to publish, and that reason is you.

Without a listener, the musician is just making noise for no one to hear. Without a hungry belly to feed, the chef has no reason to cook. And without a reader, the author cries out their thoughts to a dark and empty room. The circuit must be completed for that energy to flow properly, and you are the completion of that circuit.

Thank you, dear reader, for bringing my legacy to life as only you can.

Foreword

This was the year that I began to learn what it means to take being an author seriously, and got to work on doing the things that would show I was proud to stand behind my books. Some would say that's a strange time to tackle a new genre, and maybe a terrible time to write a bunch of books about zombies. Flesh-eating monsters may be a commonly recognized archetype these days, but they are hardly the subject of respectable literature.

At least, that's what I tried to tell these monsters when they kept showing up in my thoughts. They had different ideas, however; and the more they made their case, the more I knew I needed to write these books. I realized long ago that every story ever lived or told was made up by someone, and that both fiction and non-fiction often depend on blurry lines to fall squarely within their categories.

Also, a pretty big part of taking life seriously is having a good sense of humor. I have never had any desire to separate my inner philosopher from my inner goofball. There's certainly no reason to start now. I can't think of a better way to approach a serious subject, even if that subject is my own legacy. Or zombies.

The gravity of the messages this story had to convey were part of what won me over to writing it. Another part of it was my love of horror, and my curiosity about the deeper meaning of zombies. Yet another part was my dark sense of humor, and how many opportunities I saw for comical metaphors and telling glimpses into the human psyche in these books. For those who enjoy a fun romp through a zombie-infested world, I did my best to deliver an entertaining and enjoyable story. For those who have come to expect deeper meaning from me, my reasons for writing have never been more apparent than in these books.

I do so hope you love reading this book; I sincerely enjoyed everything that went into writing it. Perhaps by the end you will have everything you need to decide whether I am clearly taking my destiny seriously or if I am just an insufferable goofball. My hope is that you see it is actually quite a bit of both, and that you come back for more as I explore the deeper meaning of the thing I love so dearly.

It's life, by the way…the thing I love so dearly. Rather than blur the lines of fiction or non-fiction like so many writers, I pop up one big umbrella and watch everything fall neatly under it. The first time I ran across a definition of a philosopher I realized that it was defining me. Philosophy is the study of life, and I can't get enough of poking around in dark and frightful corners any more than I can get enough of tilting my face toward the sun. Now I disagree with that definition, and call it incomplete. The philosopher must do more than study life: we must live it, and love it; and laugh at both it and ourselves from time to time. Most importantly, we must share that love and that laughter in whatever way we feel called to do so.

This is my way. I take it very seriously. But I won't judge myself on your behalf; I'll leave that to you. Once again, I hope you enjoy reading 'Zombie Zero: The Last Zombie'. If you decide that you have found a serious new author that you would like to keep up on, you might want to join The Secret Society of Deeper Meaning. It's my newsletter, and it will keep you up to date about how seriously I'm taking my writing these days. It will also prove beyond the shadow of a doubt that I am indeed an insufferable goofball, and seriously touched by the dork angel.

What a strange way to be serious, hmmm?

Prologue

"I'm not here to hurt you!" Allen tried to keep the hunger out of his voice. He held up the bag of pills, shook it noisily. "I want to help!"

Allen could see the small cluster of bedraggled men on deck; he could even see the ones with scoped rifles that thought they were hiding. He could smell them all as well, but he did his best to ignore that. There was one woman in the cluster, and he could smell her most distinctly. She smelled delicious; not in a sexual sense, but in a purely cannibalistic way. One of the men on deck gave a signal, and three shots rang out. A bullet ricocheted off the water behind Allen's small rowboat with a splash. Another ripped through his shoulder; at the same time, the third punctured the boat. The force of the blow threw him backward to the floorboards.

Cold salty water splashed in his face. Allen twisted sideways, still lying down, and tried to shove a rag in the hole. Water trickled in around it, streaming in every direction from the puncture. When he didn't get up right away, a collective cry rose from the little ship.

"Idiots," he grumbled under his breath. "You can't kill a howler with bullets." He looked down at his shoulder; there was no wound, no scar, no hint that a bullet had passed through it moments earlier. Allen smiled. Being a zombie had its perks.

Allen sat up quickly and grabbed at the oars. Their voices died, and three more reports sounded. Two bullets ripped through the boat, each leaving two holes behind. One started squirting water right away; the other three would follow soon after. It appeared that every man on deck had a firearm. They'd had them holstered or shouldered as he approached; now they raised them and began firing. He couldn't see the woman anymore.

Rowing with all his might, Allen could feel the little vessel dip lower in the water. His feet were getting wet, and one more of the holes had started to stream water into the sizable puddle that had already collected. The others spurted seawater at him whenever a wave hit the side of the boat. A barrage of bullets came his way as he pushed and pulled at the oars. Most of them rained into the sea all around him, but more than one struck him soundly in the face or the ribs. Tugging on the oars was barely moving him at all, and the little boat was looking more like a little bathtub with each passing moment. The bag was floating, and Allen snatched it and tied it to his belt. More holes let in more water, and a bullet struck the clamp holding one of the oars.

It sprung from his hand, swinging wildly past his reaching grasp.

Watching the oar float away slowly, Allen banged at the other clamp in an attempt to free the remaining paddle. His razor talons were too long for him to close his fingers into a proper fist, and they bit into his palms as he beat against the metal. The water was past his ankles now, and the boat was tipping forward precariously. Another bullet glanced off his heavy brow, and Allen was laid back once again. His head splashed into the cold water, and this time he stayed down.

A few more shots sounded, and one bullet zinged past

what used to be his nose; then all was quiet. The water sent cold prickling tingles through his brain and body, and Allen took a nice deep breath as water lapped at his fleshless face. For a full minute he lay still, letting the boat sink beneath the surface and twist with the drifting current. He swam deeper, until the pressure pounded at his iron skull and the sunlight became a distant glow. Then he swam for the ship, long powerful strokes that pulled him rapidly closer.

There had never been any reason to wonder if he could survive long underwater. As he stroked toward the dark shadow on the surface above him, Allen realized that he didn't need to hold his breath. Three little slits opened up at the base of his throat, and he breathed in easily through the gills. For a moment he mused that Mother Nature had designed zombies better than people; then he realized it was so they could eat those that fled by sea, and he put his mind elsewhere. The last person he wanted to think about, now or ever again, was Mother Nature.

Once he was directly under the vessel, Allen let himself drift upward. He grasped the underside of the boat as silently as possible, sinking his claws into the wood just enough to hold him there without effort. There was no need to worry about sharks, or other underwater predators or scavengers; nature knew death when it smelled it, and they all kept far away. In a little while it would be dark, and he would board the ship and do what he could to make friends. Allen ignored the gnawing in his gut that told him that his best bet was to eat some of them.

That was just the hunger talking.

Chapter 1

"We killed that thing," Jack grumbled.

"I think you're wrong," Lauren said quietly, but firmly. "First of all, 'it' wasn't an 'it'; 'it' was a 'he'. Second, I don't think you killed him."

"Based on what?" Jack hissed.

Lauren shrugged. "Based on the fact that you weren't using cannons, or high-powered rifles. Even then, you have to shoot them in the eye exactly the right way. I'm not saying you're bad shots, or that you didn't hit him. I'm saying guns don't kill howlers."

"Bullshit!" Jack spat. "I saw it go down. It wasn't moving."

He got right up in her face, and put his hand on the butt of his revolver. Lauren let her hand hover over her holster, reminding him of the two times she had already outdrawn him. Inwardly she sighed. Jack had been nothing but trouble since she had picked him up three days ago.

"Back off," she warned. "If you don't like the way I run my ship, you are free to leave any time."

"Your ship!" he retorted. "Nothing belongs to anyone anymore. What makes this your ship?"

"The organization that I belong to made me captain," she said. "They sent me out to rescue anyone I could find. They also gave me the authority to handle any dangerous or violent refugees in any manner I see fit. That means I can kill you if I want, or put you in one of the cells below deck until all the others are filled with ramblers and howlers."

"Zombies?" Jack looked around for other frowning faces. "You want to pick up zombies?"

"I have gone over all of this with you before."

"I was dehydrated, hungry," Jack said. "I would have agreed to anything. Are you really saying there's no place for a democracy here? Your boat, your rules? What if I want to be the captain?"

"Well, first you'll have to kill me, or put me in a cell," Lauren stated calmly. "Then you would have to figure out how to override the security measures that prevent anyone but me from entering the captain's cabin or accessing the ship's control panels. You would need my live fingerprints and retinas, as well as all of my passwords."

Lauren looked him up and down, and smiled.

"I don't think you have the ability to complete any of those tasks, or get any of those things," she said lightly, "but I am kind of hoping that you try."

"Pretty brave behind your fancy quickdraw," he sneered.

Slowly, Lauren unbuckled her belt. The pistol fell to the floor.

She spread her hands. "And now?"

Jack went for his gun, and she went for his throat. A short blade appeared in her hand as she moved, and all three inches disappeared into his throat four times in the space of a breath. Jack fell to the floor, his eyes open and lifeless, and lay there unmoving. His pistol was still holstered at his hip.

Lauren knelt and retrieved her firearm. The knife had disappeared.

"Any other questions?" she asked, letting her eyes roam the room.

"Why didn't you shoot at the zombie?"

"I don't think he was a hostile," she said. "I know for

sure that the shooting began before we knew for sure. That will not happen again. The next person who draws their firearm or shoots anyone will answer to me."

Lauren looked down at what used to be Jack. She let a long moment pass before she spoke again, to give everyone a chance to see what it meant to answer to her.

"Someone cut off his head, and throw it and his body overboard," she said. "We will be looking for friendlies, howlers and ramblers and people. We will not take aggressive action unless there is a clear need, and I give a clear command. Anyone willing to help me on this mission will be greatly appreciated. Anyone who would stand in my way, or disagree with how I captain this ship, can stick to their quarters or stay out of the way. I will give you food and drinking water, but I will not tolerate any form of insubordination. Is that understood?"

Most of them murmured under their breaths, or nodded. One man stepped forward. "I second that, Captain. You'll get only support from me. Anyone who wants to challenge this brave badass young lady, come to me first. I'll see to it that you see the light, one way or another."

He towered over her, which didn't intimidate Lauren in the least. She knew that big guys who don't know how to handle themselves are as likely to get tangled up in their own long limbs as short fellows like Jack are to get caught up in their own egos. Studying him, she knew he was not one to get tangled up in himself. Lauren couldn't tell what style of fighting he had trained in, but some discipline had soaked into his every movement. To an ordinary bystander, he may have looked like a pretty open and relaxed guy. He was armed, but everyone was armed these days; often a collection of weapons strapped to a modern man or woman spoke more of superior raiding skills than any actual fighting ability. Lauren suspected every gun and blade in evidence on his body had belonged to him long before the fall.

She nodded her gratitude to him, and her respect. "I'm Lauren."

"I know," he nodded in return. "I'm Nick, Captain, and I am at your service. If you would step back a bit, I'll take care of this mess for you."

Nick unsheathed one of the long twin blades at his back. Lauren stepped back, along with the others. Her eyes went wide as the blade flashed. Three sudden strikes, and Jack's head rolled at her feet. Nick bent and picked the body up. He nodded at the head, and then at the cluster of men.

"Somebody grab that, and follow me," he said.

Two of them moved. One grabbed Jack's head by the hair, and they both trailed Nick above deck.

"Look over the side when you toss the body," she called out after them. "See if that howler is lurking nearby."

"Yes, Captain," Nick's voice drifted back to her. "Good idea."

They were back a few minutes later, and it was much less tense in the cabin with the body gone. The remaining blood had mostly soaked into the floorboards.

"No sign of him, Captain," Nick reported.

"Thank you," she responded. "Now that you're back, it might be a good time to reiterate what I told each of you when you came aboard. We will fill this vessel with friendlies, and then we will return together to safety. Then we can go back; but not until then."

"Back where?" someone asked. She couldn't remember his name. "Who exactly do you work for?"

"I don't work for anyone," Lauren answered. "The organization I belong to does not have a name. Neither does the place we are going. It was protected from the pulse, and the outbreak. It is a safe place, and we have plenty of room and food for everyone that remains. All that are willing to live without violence are welcome to stay with us as long as is necessary. It is an underground city capable of supporting several thousand people. It was built long ago by the organization I belong to, and the few hundred of us that live there are dedicated to its purpose and its upkeep."

Chapter 2

Christina watched the pile of bodies burn, saw the stinky tendril of smoke drift to the sky. She turned to look at the fresh turned soil not far from where the bodies burned, and her heart twisted in grief.

Everything had been fine until someone had died. They had all watched news reports, but the floating island had not been touched by the zombie outbreak. Then a fisherman had got caught in his own net and drowned. Death had barely closed his eyes when hunger opened them, and he had infected three others before the situation had gotten under control. They had nowhere to house prisoners, and no way to contain their hunger. As with everything on the island, it had been put to a vote.

She watched the bodies burn. It was both a relief and a horror. They had been her friends, her peers. Christina had respected every one of them enough to invite them to the drifting paradise, and they had all contributed more than their fair share. Now they were dead, twisted beheaded versions of the brilliance they once were dripping to featureless flesh in the flames. For all the times she had shared credit for her own great work, Christina felt fully to blame for their deaths.

"I know what you're thinking," Jason said quietly. They didn't look at each other. He stood at her side, staring into the flames, sharing in her sublime grief. The crackling of the fire was loud, and they were close enough to smell the stench. She had heard him over the noise of the burn and the turmoil of her thoughts, and he knew it. Even if she hadn't, she would have heard his next words.

"You're wrong," he murmured. "This is not your fault. You know what is your fault? The rest of us still being alive. Do you not see what this all means? You may have saved humanity with this island. You at least gave a few hundred of its members a fighting chance. Take responsibility for that, if you're going to take responsibility for something. Or take responsibility for me being happy and in love like I never thought possible. But not this. We voted on this. We share responsibility for this."

"We need to find some way to contain these things," she said quietly. "We need to get ahold of some of those pills. This can't happen again."

Christina felt his hand reach out to take hers. Her eyes drifted to the freshly turned pile of dirt again.

"I miss Penny," she said, even more quietly. It didn't matter. Jason didn't have to hear; he knew her thoughts.

"She was the soul of the island," she said. A tear drifted unnoticed down her cheek. "Since she died…"

"You're the soul of this island," Jason said, correcting her lovingly once more. "You keep everyone fueled with your unfailing positivity and your inexhaustible brilliance. We all need you as much as you need us."

He squeezed her hand. "Some of us more than others."

Christina nodded, turned at last to look at something other than flames or sorrow. She met every pair of eyes with her own before she raised her voice.

"This won't happen again," she said. "If another one of us falls victim to this outbreak, I want to save that member of our family. That means we need to build containment cells, and find a source for the cure. I need help. Any ideas?"

Chapter 3

Clinging to the side of the boat was easier than holding on to the bottom. It had been nice of them to drop a snack; but it had seemed a bit too much like bait to him. Allen had watched the head and body float past wistfully. He had waited till dark, waited what he thought was about another hour, then carefully scaled the side of the ship. He heard voices on deck as he approached the railing. Allen stopped, listened.

"-don't care what the little lady says," one voice said, "if I see a zombie coming at me, I'm not waiting for orders. I'm going to kill it."

Another voice laughed, spoke. "How many howlers did you kill before she rescued you?"

"None," the first admitted. "I took out quite a few ramblers, but never a howler. You? You ever kill a howler?"

"I saw one die," the man replied, serious. "I can't say I killed it. There were seven of us, armed and ready for the attack. It didn't matter. We filled that thing so full of bullets. It brushed them off like we were shooting it with squirt guns. We all had swords. We hacked at it while it ate one of us. The blades bent and broke. It ignored us until it was done eating, then it bit a couple of us. They started trying to eat the rest of us. One of the others wrapped a chain around the howler's neck and hung him, and the rest of us killed the ramblers that had been our friends less than sixty seconds before. We tried to behead the howler, climbing chains with what was left of our swords to hack at his neck."

Allen heard the man sigh. "He was not nearly as helpless as he looked up there. He got ahold of one guy and started eating him, and cut the other two to ribbons with his claws. I hacked at his head until it finally came off. By then I was the only one still alive and still human. I barely made it, out of seven trained special forces troops."

"Hey," the first man spoke again, surprise in his voice. "I didn't know you were special forces."

"I don't tell folks that anymore," the storyteller said quietly. "Not after that. I don't mess with howlers, either. I run."

"What if one gets on the ship?"

"It sounds like that's the plan," the wary voice came back. "She wants to save everyone, even the zombies. If one of those things gets onboard, and it isn't friendly, there's very little any of us can do to stop it from doing whatever it wants to do."

The men sat in what Allen hoped was thoughtful silence for a minute or two. He crept carefully to the edge of the deck, peered at their feet. They had their backs to him, and were fifteen or twenty feet away. He climbed the railing slowly, carefully, watching them. His feet hit the deck, and Allen let the landing make enough noise to alert them of his presence. They turned to the sound.

"I'm one of the good guys," he said, spreading his hands.

Both men went for their guns. Allen crossed the space between them in one leap, slapped the firearms from their hands, and leapt back.

"I don't want to hurt you," he said.

They men drew swords, one from his hip and the other from his back.

Allen grasped the bag of pills at his waist, shook it. "I'm in recovery."

They came at him. Allen had time to roll his eyes, put his hands on his hips and sigh before they reached him. When they did reach him, he was no longer there. Stepping between them as they swung sharp steel at him, Allen was behind them as their swords bit into the railing. He backed away slowly, spreading his hands before him to feign defenselessness.

One man was clearly panicked, and his sword came free first. He ran at Allen, the blade back over his head. His steps were uncertain on the shifting surface of the deck, and they drove him right into Allen's grasp. Long talons sunk into his soft belly. Allen tried to pull back, but the man fell on him bodily as his sword clattered to the deck. Another deep set of gashes appeared on his arm as he fell beside his weapon.

The smell of blood assaulted his senses, and Allen was awash in his hunger suddenly. He fell upon the bleeding man, biting at his arm and shoulder and neck. After a few moments the man stopped fighting him and embraced the violence. Allen's mouth was full of blood and warm flesh when his mind came back to him. He pushed the man away, fighting the death grip of his arms. The man grabbed the back of Allen's head, and shoved it back into the bloody mess that had been his shoulder a few moments before.

One man was holding him, the other was banging at his back with a sword, and Allen could feel his howler strength pulsing through his veins. He grasped the rambler's head, gnawed at his neck, and pulled. The blade bit into his neck from behind as the rambler's head came free in his hands. A moment later, the grip of death relaxed its hold on him.

Allen rolled onto his back. The sword was still lodged in his spine, and the remaining man was grasping the hilt;

both spun as Allen turned. They hit the deck together, and man and blade bumped and clattered away.

Leaping to his feet, Allen slipped in blood as the ship swayed. His face thudded against the deck. Before he knew it he was under attack again, crossing his arms in front of him to absorb the blows of the blade. He kicked at the man's feet, hard, and he went down. Suddenly Allen found himself staring at the man as they both lay sideways on the floorboards, facing each other. He reached out one hand, covered the man's face in flesh and talons, and squeezed.

His head burst like a melon. Allen leapt on top of him, gnawing at his neck and shoulders until his arms fell off one by one. By the time his belly was full, the corpse was a bloody mess in four bony pieces. He threw all of the body parts overboard, picked up a sword and a pistol, and moved cautiously further along the deck. It was late, and it was quiet, but he heard voices and saw lights ahead.

He also smelled fresh flesh.

Chapter 4

Lauren peered anxiously at the little vessel. It was still too far off to tell if anyone was in it yet. The sun was rising behind the other boat, making it look like it was on fire rather than simply drifting. The light reflected off the thick glass between her and the ocean air. Lauren peered through the network of wire between the two sheets of transparency at Nick's wide back. He was eyeing the drifting boat with binoculars.

Depressing the button on her radio, she asked, "See anything?"

She saw him shake his head, reach for the radio. Nick kept the field glasses up to his eyes.

"Not yet," his voice came back. "Something's moving on deck, for sure, but I can't tell what it is."

Lauren watched him watch the vessel, until he dropped the binoculars and turned to meet her eyes through the grated glass. She could see the horror in his eyes, and the fear. Bringing the radio to his lips, he spoke quietly into it.

"Captain," he murmured, "it's all howlers. I saw at least a dozen."

Nick hesitated, lowering the radio while he held her gaze. Shaking his head, he raised the device to his mouth once more.

"They're eating each other," he added quietly.

Lauren eased up on the throttle, thumbed the button

on her radio.

"Could you come in here please?" she asked.

Nick disappeared. A minute later, there was a knock on the door. Lauren locked the wheel and backed the throttle off even further. Crossing the cabin in a few steps, she keyed the pad next to the door. A screen lit up next to the keypad, glowing faintly red. She placed her thumb over it until it beeped, then moved her right eye to be scanned. The soft beep sounded again, and the door clicked open.

Ushering him inside, she closed the door swiftly behind him. Lauren went back to the wheel, but she didn't unlock it or fiddle with the throttle any more. Instead she peered out the window, squinting against the sunrise. Nick came to stand beside her, and share her view.

"They weren't eating each other before," she said.

Nick nodded his agreement. "They are now."

"You're sure?"

He held the field glasses out to her. "You should be able to see for yourself by now."

"I'm not doubting your word." Lauren made no move to take them.

"I'm not saying you are," he shrugged. "I wouldn't believe it if I hadn't seen it either. I would want to see for myself."

He pressed the glasses into her hands, smiling.

Lauren took them, put them to her eyes. She frowned, forcing herself to watch until she was absolutely certain. A shudder ran through her body. Handing the binoculars back to Nick, she looked up at him.

"There are cannons below deck," she said. "They're very easy to use, and anyone with half a mind can be trained to fire them with accuracy in less than a minute. Do you know of six or eight men or women with half a mind or better on this vessel?"

"Aye, Captain," he grinned. "I can round up more than that, at least twice as many. Two are still missing, the men I had posted as guards night before last. I keep hoping they'll turn up, but I don't need them for this. Most of the women are in their cabins, and some of the men too; but they seem like a reasonable bunch for the most part."

"You've spoken with everyone?" Lauren arched an eyebrow.

"Almost," he shrugged. "I kind of fancy myself your first mate. I hope that's okay. I have knocked on every door, approached everyone that comes out at mealtimes, and asked if they needed anything. Most said no, but to tell you thank you. Most of them also said that if you need any help, they will be there for you. I don't imagine any bad guys being daft enough to come up to me and say, 'Hey, I'm a subversive', but everyone seems pretty well put together."

Lauren let her eyes move to the window again. "Leave it to a good apocalypse to leave only the finest standing," she muttered.

"It's true," Nick agreed. "Most of the men on board have some military background, and many of the women do as well. Everyone seems to have some valid real-life experience in dealing with harsh reality of one sort or another. They're shaken, but they're sound."

"Did you get a count?" she asked.

He nodded.

"Twenty-six men and eight women?"

He nodded again. "Minus the two missing."

"No children?"

Nick shook his head. "No kids. What's your capacity?"

"Our capacity," she smiled, "is two to three hundred humans and about fifty or sixty howlers. We have room for twice as many of them, and medicine, but only if they bunk together."

"That's out," he said, echoing her earlier shudder.

Lauren nodded. "Can you stop a half dozen people from shooting unless commanded to?"

"I think so," Nick answered. "I'll do my damnedest."

"Alright." Lauren tapped a few panels on the dash. They continued to drift toward the other craft, but more slowly. She crossed the cabin and accessed the exit.

"That's serious security," Nick noted. "Why on the inside?"

Lauren didn't look back over her shoulder, speaking as she walked.

"In case someone chops off my hand and cuts out my eye," she said blithely. "They won't be able to use them after awhile. The controls automatically take my fingerprints continually as I use them, and some prompts are voice activated. The cabin becomes a prison for anyone who gets inside of it that isn't me. The ventilation system releases a sedative gas, and the ship's autopilot takes it home."

"That's quite a ventilation system," he said.

"It does more than that." Lauren stopped at a door and went through another security sequence. "It also filters any kind of air, from nuclear fallout to chemical gas to minor pollutants. If there's no breathable atmosphere for some reason, it has plenty of oxygen to pressurize the cabin for several weeks. Belowdeck is the same."

"All of it?" Nick followed her into the room, watched her access another control board. Six panels opened in the wall, and six cannons moved on mechanical tracks to poke their barrels through the holes.

"All of it," she answered. "Come here, please."

She took his hand, gently, and placed it over the control panel. It beeped, and she nodded in its general direction.

"Put your eye over the screen," she said.

Nick moved to position his right eye over the glowing

panel, opening it wide. It beeped again.

"Thank you," she said. "Type in your name on the number pad, six-four-two-five, then put in your hand print and retina scan. You will be able to get in most of the security doors on the ship using that sequence. You will also be able to activate, control and deactivate certain security measures. Try it."

Nodding to the screen again, she stepped back. Nick keyed the code, scanned his hand and eye, and read the screen.

"'First Mate'," he read, smiling. "That's quite a menu."

"Select 'cannons'," she said.

Nick pressed the lighted section with the image of a cannon. A new menu appeared. It gave him the options of activating or stowing the weapons, individually or collectively.

"Select 'activate cannon six'," she said.

He pressed another section of the screen. The rounded end of the nearest cannon moved from the cushioned seat to thrust even further through the portal. The glass targeting ring began to glow with a green light. Lauren motioned him to the seat behind the triggered handles. Settling in, Nick moved the wide barrel until the site was on the other ship. It went yellow as he neared the vessel, and red as he found it.

"See?" she said. "Simple."

"Can I keep the cannons in safety mode with gunners at the ready?"

Lauren shook her head. "No. Once a cannon is activated…"

She trailed off.

"Not so simple after all," he pointed out.

Nick got up, went to the panel and deactivated all of the cannons. They slid back into their stored position, and the panels moved back into place. He moved to the door, punched in the sequence, and opened it for her.

"I have some gunners to round up," he said. "And I believe you have a ship to hail."

"Keep your radio on."

"Always," he smiled. "Be careful up there."

Chapter 5

There were four lifeboats held in reserve on the ship. The smallest was as vacant as the other three, and more than big enough for Allen to set up a zombie sanctuary. He'd taken another pill, stripped off his bloodstained clothes, and laid in a bunk waiting for the hunger to go away. He felt like a junkie, lying there silently while the day went on below. The sounds of voices and footsteps drifted up to the lifeboat all day, along with whiffs of flesh and sweat. All he had to do was grab one of them and start eating, and he would reverse the transformation once again. The hunger gnawed at him, and he fantasized about eating someone like he had once fantasized about being with someone.

On the morning of the second day, he heard a different kind of commotion on deck. It started out as uneasy murmurs, and Allen had to strain to hear. Minutes later, people were shouting and swearing; he peeked his eyes over the side of the boat to see.

There was a craft half the size of theirs drifting toward them. Someone was either captaining the ship to keep it exactly three hundred feet away, or the autopilot was amazing. Allen watched, and listened.

"Ahoy!" A woman was talking through a bullhorn, the same woman he had seen on deck when he had approached in his little rowboat. He could smell her too; the scent was as alive and intoxicating as the fear of the others.

Allen had a pretty good vantage point from where he stood. He could see the deck of the other boat. It was crawling with howlers, and covered in blood. They were tearing each other to pieces, and then they were eating the pieces. He shuddered, sank back to the floorboards. There were dozens of them, although it looked as though there had been twice that a couple of days earlier. Every square inch of the deck was painted in gore, dried and crusted or fresh and slick. Allen's stomach clenched in hunger.

"We have the cure!" The woman was still trying to get their attention. "Ahoy! Anyone willing to be locked up until you become human again is welcome on our ship! We have the cure!"

Allen peeked over the side, got a good look at her face. She looked frustrated; she had taken the amplifier from her lips, and had her hands on her hips. She was frowning. He edged back, turned his gaze to the other deck. The howlers were oblivious, fighting for their lives and for a scrap of food.

The woman pulled a pistol from her hip, pointed it in the air. She put the megaphone to her mouth again. "This is not an aggressive action. No one on this vessel is authorized to discharge a weapon of any kind at this time. I am trying to get their attention. I repeat, do not fire on the boat."

Stealing another glance over the edge of the lifeboat, Allen saw that everyone on deck was armed. He shook his head. Those rifles and pistols were not enough.

A shot rang out. Allen backed further into his sanctuary, still watching the other deck. The howlers had heard it too. A few of them disengaged from the feeding frenzy to glance over the railing. One howl split the air, and a dozen answered immediately. Soon the railing was lined with zombies, looking at the ship and howling their hunger.

"I repeat," the woman said into the megaphone, "we have the cure. Anyone willing to tolerate temporary incarceration while we administer the cure is welcome aboard. The transformation only takes a few days. You can all be human again. We will…no, wait! Don't jump!"

By the time she had said the words, four howlers had leapt into the water. Three disappeared beneath the waves, while the fourth began to stroke powerfully across the water towards them. A dozen more leapt over the railing, and Allen shook his head again.

"You are not authorized to approach this ship," the woman's amplified voice came once more. "Turn back, and allow us to process you individually. Approaching us without authorization will be considered an aggressive act, and we will retaliate."

She unclipped a radio from her belt, and Allen imagined all the ways this might play out. Every scenario he imagined ended in one ship or the other sinking or empty, at best; either all of the howlers or all of the humans would be lost. He sighed.

Leaping over the side of the lifeboat, he landed right next to the woman on the deck. Allen snatched the megaphone from her hand and put it to the sparse flesh of his lips.

"Stay on your boat if you want to live!" he shouted into the device. "Turn back now if you're in the water!"

He dropped the megaphone and turned to her. "Get your people out of here!" Then he leapt over the railing. He hit the water hard.

Allen felt weak, hungry. He let himself sink for a minute. He had seen the cannons poking out the side of the boat as he passed; he was glad to note that they were not so defenseless after all. No shots had rang out as he had fallen alongside the ship; no bullets sank beside him in the water. Unfortunately, the ship was not moving away either.

One howler was close, and so bent on climbing the side of the ship that it did not see Allen swim up behind it. Sinking his teeth into her shoulder, he wrenched her from her moorings as his strength came back to him. He invaded her mind with his own, observing her thoughts for a moment. She was all hunger, consumed with it and identified by it; he tore her head off.

Stroking across the surface of the water, Allen felt eyes and scopes on him. The knowledge of the cannons did little to comfort him now, but there was no time to think on that; two howlers were climbing the side of the vessel. He didn't have to touch their minds to know their intentions: they stopped every time they sank their talons into the hull, and howled their hunger. The first one was easy to grab, and pull back into the water; Allen removed his head with three giant bites. The second saw Allen approaching, and started climbing faster. He had to leap through the air to catch him by the ankle.

The monster dug into the side of the ship, trying to kick him loose. Allen caught his ankle in his mouth, and bit off his foot in one huge bite. Hot blood filled his mouth, fresh strength filled his muscles, and he got his own legs under him against the hull. Allen pushed off with all of his might, and they swung together to smash against hard metal. He looked up, saw that the long sharp claws of one of the creature's hands had been torn off. They protruded from the side of the ship, dripping blood.

Allen kicked off again, and this time they fell together into the water. He felt teeth sink into his arm as his gills opened, and used the leverage to get behind his attacker. Wrapping his legs around the monster's torso, Allen crossed his free arm over the mangled one. He pulled back with all of his might, locking those scissoring jaws open. Diving in with his own rows of jagged teeth, Allen ate most of one shoulder and his neck as they drifted slowly deeper in the water. The body finally went limp in his clutches, and Allen let it go to float away in pieces.

From here, he could see how many more were in the water. He could hear their thoughts; they were nothing but hunger. Allen stroked for the surface; by the time his gills closed, his arm was whole again. Taking a breath, his head just out of the water, his eyes went round.

They were cheering. The people on the deck had been watching, waiting to see if he prevailed. When he broke the surface, they had recognized him. And they were cheering him.

Allen fought back a tear; he knew it would just drip down his face as a drop of blood if he shed it. He raised his arms over his head and waved them frantically.

"Get out of here!" he screamed.

Another howler reached the ship. It started climbing. Allen stroked towards it, skimming through the waves to seize his ankle. He tugged, and the howler fell into the water with him. The ship was still not moving. Allen grasped the howler by the arm and pulled himself under the surface. While chomping through sinew and spine he looked around under the water, and reached out with his mind. He could hear their fevered single-minded thinking, and feel their hunger. There were too many. They had gone under and around the ship, and a half dozen of them were climbing the hull or preparing to.

Spitting out a mouthful of blood and water, Allen took another deep breath as his gills sealed shut. He looked up, saw eyes peering over the railing to watch him. They were cheering him still, and he was shouting again.

"Get out of here!" he hollered once more. "You're being boarded!"

He couldn't see the woman that had been speaking for the vessel. Allen pulled another howler from the hull and swam under the ship. Finally, it began to move. He watched the bottom of the vessel drifting by overhead, and Allen had to swim upward to latch on before it moved past him completely. Pulling against the rushing water, he clambered along the horizontal hull until his path turned vertical.

Finally pulling himself free of the water, Allen saw a howler jump over the railing above him, and another nearly completing the climb. There were a half dozen trails of talon marks leading up this side of the ship, and no cannons. Gunshots rang out overhead, and he began his hurried ascent just as the last howler cleared the railing. Screaming and howling and gunfire filled his ears as he climbed.

Chapter 6

Lauren watched through the thick grated glass as one howler after another leapt to the deck and started taking people down. She had hurried to the cabin as quickly as she could, cursing and pounding the wall as she went through the interminable security protocols. Racing to the controls at last, she had maxed out the throttle and locked the wheel. In the next moment her radio was in her hand.

"Howlers on deck. Report to the cabin. Bring your gunners," she hissed into it. Clipping it back on her belt, she crossed the room to access another control panel. It slid open just as pounding sounded on the door. Lauren grasped one of the pistols from the rack of weapons, trained it on the door while she went through the security sequence. Pulling it open, her heart pounding, she sighed as she saw Nick's troubled countenance. A half dozen others stood behind him, looking equally concerned. Lauren lowered the pistol.

Standing aside, she pointed at the row of firearms.

"These are serious weapons," she said. "The pistols are fifty caliper, and they are loaded with shrapnel rounds designed to explode on impact. The rifles have actual explosive charges in the bullets. They can damage the hull of this ship. Use them with extreme caution."

Nick stood by her side while the others gathered weapons.

"One of them is helping us," Lauren pointed out. "Don't shoot him."

A man frowned, hefting a rifle. "How do we tell them apart?"

"He's the one helping us," Nick said sharply. "The howler that is attacking other howlers is not to be shot. The howlers that are attacking our shipmates must be shot only when you have considered what is behind them and all around them. Is that clear?"

They all nodded.

"Then go get some." He grinned as they filed out. Nick moved to grasp a rifle, his hand falling on the same one Lauren was reaching for. Their fingers touched, for a moment; then she drew back. Grabbing a different weapon, she pulled it from its place.

"You should stay down here," Nick frowned.

Lauren shook her head. "You think I can't handle myself?"

Nick chuckled. "Against a howler, Captain? I have yet to meet any human who can handle themselves against a howler. I'm not being protective, Captain. All personal feelings aside, I don't think the most important person on the ship should engage in combat of any kind. We need you to lead more than we need you to fight."

Lauren shook her head. "If I don't fight, I can't lead. It's why I'm trained in both. Come on, we're wasting time."

He followed her out of the cabin, watched her smile as she hesitated at the door that would lead them to the deck. She opened her mouth, to say something. The door exploded inward, tossing pieces of wood and metal at both of them. Lauren took the brunt of the impact, and swung with the remainder of the door until they struck the wall together. Nick found himself standing face to face with a monster. Her rows of teeth were dripping blood, her talons covered in gore. Whatever clothes she had once worn were now rags painted in shades of red.

Nick stumbled backward, setting his rifle aside to unsheathe his sword. He only barely got it out before she tackled him to the ground and started biting at his face. The sword was trapped between them, and he was holding it against her throat with everything he had. It wasn't sharp enough, and he wasn't strong enough, and her teeth kept getting closer to his face.

A loud report sounded, and her body was thrown off him sideways. The howler launched to her feet, her skull exposed and bloody on one side. She turned to Lauren where she stood over Nick and howled hunger and anger at her. Lauren squeezed the trigger on her pistol three more times. The rest of the monster's head turned to red and white paste, and drifting spaghetti. The rest of her toppled bodily on top of Nick.

Shoving her off, he took the hand Lauren proffered him and got his feet under him again. Nick sheathed his sword and retrieved his rifle.

"Careful," Lauren grinned. "All personal feelings aside, I need you alive."

She didn't give him time to respond. Lauren breezed through the doorway, pistol before her. She was crouched, and hugging the wall, so he stood tall and aimed over her. As they came around the corner, their weapons fired as one. Another howler burst into a cloud of bloody bits, as did a section of the railing.

"Go easy with that thing," she said, glancing back at him.

Nick laughed. "I'm pretty sure you took out the railing."

He swiveled at a sudden movement, trained his sights on it.

Lauren put a hand on his arm.

"Don't," she said. "That's him."

The howler streaked past them to tackle another as it climbed onto the deck. They rolled together on the planking, sprays of red and pieces of flesh flying as they scratched and bit.

Nick was transfixed, watching; Lauren nudged him.

"Let's stick by him," she murmured. "We might need to protect him when this is all over."

His pistol was in his hand, and he hollered.

"Get down!"

Both monsters were vicious, and fast; but one was more calculated in its movements. It glanced over, grabbed the other creature's neck and held it high. The howler scraped at him with razor talons, painting the deck in his blood, as its head was held firmly still in place. Whatever time it took for Nick to take aim was wildly distorted from all of their points of view: it seemed a scant second for Nick, long breathless moments to Lauren, and a lifetime to their unlikely ally. At last the creature's head exploded, along with a part of the friendly howler's hand.

He rolled, got on top of the monster and began feeding. In moments his torso was whole again, and his hand had sprouted fresh fingers. As he lifted his head from the bite, the howler smiled in grisly gratitude. It streaked away, and they ran to follow.

Lauren stopped to take aim before the howler struck it; when they tumbled to a tangled heap, it was as if the creature was reading her mind. He lifted the other howler clear of his body, his back to the deck, and she took off its head. Nick was almost upon the melee as the skull burst in front of him, and he kept running as the howler streaked along the deck to its next victim. They cleared the deck in minutes, leapfrogging each other and taking steady sure shots. When the last monster went down, they got on both sides of their ally and guarded him while he fed.

"Thank you," Lauren called out, over her shoulder. Her shipmates were beginning to approach, cautiously. She tried to ignore the sounds of fevered feeding behind her, hoping they would stop before the others were close enough to hear.

"Stay back!" Nick was not willing to take the chance, apparently. He walked a wide brisk circle around Lauren and the creature, waving his pistol. "This howler just saved all of our lives. The captain will need some time with him, and then we will carry out whatever orders she has for us. In the meantime, put your weapons away. Stay back, and don't make me repeat myself."

Nick's sights trained on one man. He was not the only one slow in putting away his gun, but he could only point the weapon in one direction. The pistol disappeared into its holster, followed by all the others in sight.

"Good." Nick glanced at Lauren. She nodded, approached the feeding monster slowly.

"Thank you," she said again. "My name is Lauren; I'm the captain of this ship."

The howler lifted his head from the ravaged body cavity, wiped blood from his lips with the back of his hand. He nodded.

"I'm Allen," he said. "I'm here to help."

Chapter 7

One of her companions was calm, watchful; the other was anxious, and frowning fiercely. The anxious one spoke.

"Can we go any faster?"

Six eyes watched the monitor, the image of a series of hand-hewn boats following them across the water. The boats were filled with howlers, two or three in each boat. There were a dozen boats, maybe more. The monsters were paddling frantically, hungrily. They were visibly closing the gap.

Christina shook her head. "The island is designed to drift, not be driven. We have to ride the currents wherever we find them. Under our own power we can't go any faster than this."

They sat in collective silence for another minute, watching the slow predatory gain, until she spoke once more.

"We'll pick up speed soon," Christina said, pointing at another screen in the bank. It had digitized streams of information crossing it, currents and tides in different colors. Their island was a green floating blip in the middle of the readout. "We're almost to that drift. It will take us deeper into the Atlantic, headed for the Americas. We'll find the cure there."

"And weapons," he added.

Christina turned to him.

"And weapons," she echoed. "Weapons to be used defensively, in accordance with the code of this island. I know you are suffering from a painful loss, but our new weapons will not be your opportunity for revenge. There will be no unnecessary blood shed on my watch."

"Miss McMullen, that should be put to a vote."

The men stood on either side of her, watching the monitors. At his words the other man stepped back, turned to fix his eyes on the one that had spoken.

"Gary," he said. "We already voted on that, when the project began. You were brought on as security because we needed it on the open sea. What happened to your wife was terrible, and we all feel as though we lost family. That doesn't change what we stand for."

Christina nodded, her eyes never leaving the screens.

"If anything," she said. "It cements what we stand for. The world doesn't need violence now; it needs hope. We're going to do whatever we can to give it to them."

She nudged him playfully. "And what happened to 'Christina'?"

Gary's eyes went back to watching, and Jason moved to her side once more. She reached out her hand, to squeeze her husband's.

"I'm scared, Christina," Gary murmured, quietly.

She nodded.

"We're all scared, Gary," she answered. "That's okay. It's not okay to turn into a bunch of ruthless savages because most of the rest of the world has."

Jason and Gary's eyes were locked on the feed showing the approaching doom. It was hard to tell what part of the world the rowing monsters had come from; they were indigenous, their boats made from trees fallen by hand and vines wrapped and tied with care. The closest boats showed the monstrous faces aboard clearly, with their hungry hanging jaws and rows of jagged teeth.

Three of the other screens alternated between public spaces on the island, one showed muted world news recordings. Christina's eyes went between the digital readout and the boats.

"Didn't you write a book about the zombie apocalypse?" Gary asked, returning her friendly nudge. "'Going Green', wasn't it?"

Jason laughed.

"Proceeds from that book went to putting up the downtown area," he said, still chuckling. "That's why main street is called 'Green Street'. That, and because Christina was vocally opposed to calling it 'Zombie Avenue'. She only grumbled when someone came up with 'Green Street', and voted against it. We knew it was because she didn't want credit, once again, and voted her down."

"I'm right here," Christina frowned, her eyes locked on the screen.

"Thank God for that," Gary mumbled. Jason nodded.

"Was there a solution?" Gary sounded hopeful. "In your book, I mean? Sorry, I'm not a horror fan. I'm more of a 'Rise of the Discordant' kind of guy. You are still going to finish the next one this month, right?"

"Gary, ease up," Jason muttered. "She's kind of busy trying to save the world right now."

"Stop it, both of you," Christina flushed. "I'm doing what I can to keep us safe, that's all. I'm not trying to save the world. If I was, I would be doing a terrible job. There was not a solution in my zombie book; my plan for a zombie apocalypse was always to hide and hope the internet still worked."

She leaned forward, to have a closer look at the digital display. The men caught each other's eyes over her bent form, shared a smile.

"You weren't in your zombie book, I'll bet," Gary mused. "If you had been, you would have found a solution. You are the person that made the first completely self-sustaining seasteading community, the first to be recognized as a sovereign state."

"Which went on to be more than self-sustaining," Jason nodded. "We now provide food with a complete amino acid profile to thousands of people who were starving a few years ago."

"Not anymore," Christina reminded him. "Now we are on the run from flesh-eating zombies. This is not a problem I can solve, you guys. I would need to do what I did with 'Hope Island', and bring together the right minds to work on a solution. I don't know how to find those people, except to find the cure."

"Oh, good," Gary sighed. "Then you are working on a plan to save the world. You had me scared for a minute there."

She shot him a venomous glance. It didn't hide the love that she had, for him and every other member of the community. They went back to watching the feed, seeing the features of the monsters come clearer as the boats inched closer. A light on the control panel went from red to orange to green, and Christina nodded.

"We just caught it," she said. "Did you feel it?"

Gary raised an eyebrow; both men shook their heads.

"Feel what?" Jason asked.

"The island's netting just caught the stream," she grinned, pointing at the digitized display. "We'll really start moving here in a minute."

They all watched the bank of screens, her eyes locked on the drift display while they watched the monsters begin to inch away.

"Whoa," Christina spoke again, her eyes going wide.

"Did you feel that? We're picking up some serious speed."

They shook their heads again, their eyes glued to the screen. Some of the howlers had realized that the gulf between them was widening visibly; they were clambering over the side of the boats, swimming for the island. Many of the boats tilted and tipped when they leapt out, and soon the water behind the drifting seastead was thick with monsters.

"Aren't there motion stabilizers?" Gary asked, still staring at the screen. "You shouldn't be able to feel the pull of the drift."

Jason laughed, looked at his wife.

"She feels everything on this island," he said. "And she's almost never wrong, about anything."

"We are getting further away," Gary noted, nodding at the screen. "I'm glad she was right about that. Those things are terrifying."

"Those things used to be human," Christina reminded him. "As human as you or I; they can be again, with the cure. They are not the enemy until we have to defend ourselves from them. Even then, we capture them if we can. Killing is a last resort, now and always."

"Of course," Gary nodded, watching the ocean behind them become a calm and clear expanse of water once more. The zombies dwindled to dots, followed by their handmade crafts. Then they were gone. "They just freak me out, that's all."

Jason nodded his agreement.

"I know," Christina murmured. "Me too."

Chapter 8

The hunger was just hunger now. Allen didn't feel drawn to eat like he had before, like it was some higher calling that he had to fulfill. The only thing he was filling now was his belly, and the hunger didn't care that it was howler flesh filling it. With the deeper meaning gone, his guilt was gone as well; Allen drowned in the taste and the texture of it, noting to himself at some point that howlers tasted a touch gamey next to their human counterparts.

The flesh was tougher, and leaner; but it was still flesh. His teeth delighted in tearing it to pieces as much as his stomach thrilled in turning it to power for him to wield against more monsters. With one purpose gone from his hunger, Allen let another replace it. He tore through the other creatures with an abandon he had not given into before. When he knew that the next was the last, he took his time devouring as much of its flesh as he could possibly consume.

It was several glorious minutes before he realized there was a crowd gathered, watching him feed. One approached, the woman that had been holding the megaphone earlier. Allen kept his face in the other monster's hollowed out ribcage for a long moment, chewing the last mouthful and swallowing. He heard her speak through the wet gnashing sound of his own powerful jaws, chewed faster.

"Thank you," she said. "My name is Lauren. I'm the captain of this ship."

Allen swallowed the mass of sinew, lifted his head from the corpse. He wiped the blood from his face as best he could.

"I'm Allen," he said. "I'm here to help."

"I can see that," she nodded, relaxing visibly. "Thank you again."

She stepped back, turned away from him. Her hand had been far from her holstered pistol a moment ago; now it rested on its handle. Allen did not miss the motion; he suspected he wasn't the only one.

"The howlers took me by surprise," she called out. "We would have done our best against them, but many of us may have been lost if not for this man. He might look like one of them, but he fought for us. He saved us, and contained a situation I let get out of control. He deserves our respect, and our gratitude."

It was eerily quiet for a moment; Allen watched her while she watched them. He was terribly impressed with her for not even glancing at him, as if there was no threat there. Of course, the big fellow with the small armory strapped to him hadn't taken his eyes off Allen; he suspected that any attempt on her life would mean a swift end to his own. He met the man's eyes in the silence; the man gave him a curt nod, and the corner of his mouth lifted in a slight smile.

Then someone started to clap, and the spell was broken. Voices were raised in quiet shouts, then loud whoops. The sound of applause rolled across the deck to find Allen's ears; he stood to attention at the noise, and fought the bloody tears that tried to fill his eyes. People began to come close, to gather around him; Allen backed away in alarm.

"I'm contagious," he said, voicing half of his concern. "Stay back."

Lauren moved between the crowd and Allen.

"Give him space, folks," she said. "Trying to shake his

hand could result in you losing a finger, and I don't think anyone wants that. I realize all of you are grateful, and I am sure he appreciates the appreciation. But our friend has had a hard journey, made harder by us, and he could probably use some rest."

She spoke over her shoulder.

"Can I show you your quarters, friend?"

Allen nodded. "As long as its secure."

She turned, motioned to the man that had been watching them both.

"Nick," she said. "This is Allen. Let's get him somewhere safe."

Allen shook his head, lowered his voice.

"Not safe for me," he said. "Safe for them. I need to be locked up. In a few hours-"

"You'll be consumed by hunger," Lauren cut him off, speaking in tones as hushed as his, "and unable to resist the temptation of fresh flesh. I know. That's what I meant by safe. We have comfortable quarters for you, that you will not be able to escape from. We also have pills to rehabilitate you. Both are required of any howler wanting to stay aboard, even those that have helped us. Although you are the first. Can you tell me why?"

Allen looked at Nick.

"Is she always so to the point?" he asked.

Nick laughed, nodded.

"She is," he said. "I find it rather refreshing. Now, let's get you downstairs."

Allen nodded, walked between them. He pointed at a hanging lifeboat.

"I brought some pills aboard," he said. "They're in one of your lifeboats. I think it's that one."

Lauren's eyes went round. "Are they the new ones?"

Allen shook his head. "New? What do you mean?"

"What color are they?" she pressed him.

"Purple," Allen shrugged. "Why?"

"Ours are red; the new ones work faster," Lauren said, visibly relieved. "How many do you have?"

He shrugged again. "Several bottles. A couple hundred, at least."

Nick took a few strides more quickly than they did, opening a door that led belowdeck for them. Lauren paused in the doorway, looked up at him.

"I don't think Allen is going to eat me between here and his new quarters," she said. "Would you please have someone find those pills, and bring them to me? My people have been trying to get our hands on them since we heard there was a faster formula. This is a big win."

"Aye, Captain." Nick nodded, closed the door after them.

Allen spoke as soon as the door shut.

"Your people?" he echoed. "Who are your people?"

"We are an organization that is dedicated to the preservation of humanity," she answered blithely. "My turn. When did howlers start eating each other?"

Allen tried to make his smile as friendly as possible, and keep the ghastly out of it.

"A few days ago," he answered. "You know he likes you too, right?"

Lauren started walking.

"Don't be silly," she said over her shoulder. "What does the hive mind look like now?"

Allen had started walking when she did, fell easily into step beside her. At her question, he stopped.

"You sure know a lot about zombies," he said.

Lauren paused in her path, turned to meet his gaze. "We have known about this threat for some time now. This is one of the possibilities that we have been preparing for.

We have studied the phenomenon."

"At your facility?" Allen gaped. "Firsthand?"

"No," she laughed. "We made that mistake once, a long time ago. We abandoned that facility when we realized what howlers can do, and started over elsewhere. Now you know why I ask what the hive mind looks like currently. Please answer my question."

Allen nodded, started moving again.

"It's still there," he said, falling into step beside her once more. "It has changed, though. The primary directive force is gone. The hive mind is buzzing with hunger now, and that's all. There was a sense of camaraderie and unity before; when our tastes changed, that all fell away. Now the hive mind is like an open channel with nothing but static. Even the strong ones are getting weaker; they aren't exactly easy to kill, but they are definitely getting easier."

Lauren stopped before a lighted panel, put her hand on the reader and typed some numbers on the keypad. She opened a door, held it while she spoke again.

"Can you still look into the minds of other howlers?"

Allen nodded. "If I try."

"Can you tell when they are nearby?"

He nodded again.

Lauren moved through the door, held it for him to follow. The short hallway led to another security door; beyond it were cells, lining both sides of the hallway until it terminated in a steel wall.

"Each of these cells has a panic button in it," she told him, keying open the first cell on the left. She pointed to the simple red button on the wall. Allen moved into the space, before she asked him to. "Will you press it if you feel howlers approaching?"

Allen settled his weight on the bunk, bounced slightly on the comfortable softness.

"I'll try," he said, looking up at her. "There's a problem here though, Captain. If I start taking the pills again, and turning back, I won't be able to help you with that."

Lauren moved into the space with him, frowned.

"Of course," she mused. "Dammit."

"That's not all," Allen added. "I'm already starting to feel hungry again. It won't be long until I can barely inhabit my own mind, much less watch for others. Whether I take the pills or not, I can only help you if…"

He trailed off. Allen watched her nod, slowly, and gave her immense credit for not backing away from him. Her scent filled his nostrils, the hunger twisted at his belly, and she spoke again.

"If you feed regularly," Lauren finished his thought. "We could bring you the rest of the howlers still on deck. We could store the bodies in our freezers, thaw enough every few hours to keep you fed until we encounter more like them."

The hunger became disgust at the thought. Allen shook his head.

"I can't eat anything but fresh flesh," he said quietly. "My body rejects everything else. It can be howler, or it can be human; but it has to be fresh. I'm sorry, Captain. You should go."

She moved through the open door, turned on the other side to secure the opening. Lauren spoke through the thick reinforced steel bars.

"I'll bring you some of those pills, then," she said.

"Keep them," he countered. "I said it would be difficult to help. I didn't say I wasn't going to try. The pills won't turn me all the way back anyway. That's something we should talk about, when you have time. I'm not like other howlers."

Lauren nodded. "So I gather. That's why I asked before,

why you helped us. I've seen howlers help other howlers, and even ramblers; I've never seen one help humans. I'm grateful, but I'm still baffled."

Rising slowly, Allen moved to stand near the bars. He looked down at her fearless gaze, smiled without showing too many teeth.

"You've turned before," he said, holding her eyes with his. "That's why you know so much about howlers."

Lauren did not look away.

"You're right," she admitted. "I don't remember much, though. Just hunger like I've never known before, and the sublime sensation of swallowing fresh flesh."

Now she looked away.

"That's all there is to it," Allen muttered. "We're designed to need the most horrible thing there is to need, to turn the greatest predator into helpless prey. Don't feel bad if that is all you remember; there is nothing more to the experience than that. All of the body's chemical responses are geared toward that, and heightened considerably. Eating people is better than anything in the spectrum of human experience; it feels divine to the howler. That's why it's so hard to turn back. You don't just remember what you did; you remember how it felt to do it. You know that the only way to feel that again is to become that monster, and feed."

"Have you turned back?" Lauren asked him.

"I've started to, a couple times," Allen laughed. "I haven't made it all the way, but I got pretty far once. That's when I learned that I can't turn back completely. A little part of this will always be with me. The same thing that makes me different makes me the only person left that will never shake this curse. I'll keep trying, if you want; but it will likely be a waste of pills. Pills that you could use on people that actually have hope."

"There's always hope," Lauren admonished him.

It seemed an automatic response.

"When did you join your group?" he asked.

"I didn't," she frowned. "I was born into it. We all are. My parents belonged to the order, and their parents before them. We are given opportunity to live in the outside world when we reach adulthood, for a period of time; we are also given the option of leaving the order, and never returning. It is very rare that anyone leaves. Most don't even go out into the world; they consider our work too important."

Allen nodded. "Sounds pretty important to me. What do you call yourselves?"

"The order," Lauren shrugged. "We have corporate entities to build and shelter out holdings, but members don't identify with them. There is very little ego in living for the preservation of humanity."

Another automatic response, a programmed mantra that she had obviously heard and said many times before.

Allen nodded his agreement.

"Did you try it?" he asked. "Living in the outside world?"

Lauren bit her lip.

"No," she muttered. "I never had the chance. I'm only sixteen."

"You're kidding me." Allen tried to look more closely, without making her uncomfortable. "You're the most adult person I've ever met."

She didn't respond; Lauren shifted under his gaze, looking both pleased and displeased with his assessment of her. Allen's laughter died, and he shook his head.

"Does Nick know that?" he asked quietly.

Chapter 9

Angela lifted the hatch for the first time in days, pulled a full breath of fresh air deep into her lungs. She looked down the ladder, smiled.

"I told you," she said. "They're all gone."

"Let me see," a voice drifted up. "Come down."

Angela shook her head.

"No," she said, lifting the hatch further. "I'm going to check on the garden. Come on."

The voice give her pause, drifting up to her again.

"You should let me go out first."

She laughed.

"Just come on, Isaac," she said, swinging the hatch all the way open. "You can't do any more damage to a howler than I can. It doesn't matter which of us goes first. It's very sweet and all but…"

Angela climbed the last of the stairs, stood in the cool morning air. Isaac was beside her a few seconds later, a machete slid through his belt.

"Careful with that," she cautioned. "Hospitals are cemeteries now."

Isaac smiled as he stepped past her, came up on the garden first.

"Ah, honey…" he said, pulling the machete free. "Hang on."

Angela felt her eyes go wide.

"What?" she demanded. "Is it the tomatoes? Or the roses? Please don't tell me the zombies destroyed my rose garden."

Isaac shook his head.

"No," he said. "But there is a zombie in your rose garden. Be careful."

Her breath caught in her throat as she saw it, her eyes going even wider. Angela reached out, to take the blade from him.

Shaking his head, Isaac turned and moved to the gate. It stood open, and much of the food had been picked from vines that had been laden with fruit a week ago. Angela took note, and didn't mind; that meant she had helped humans survive another day. Score one for us. From the looks of the bare foliage, score several for us. She smiled as she watched Isaac approach the monster, glad she had helped. Now that she was out of that hole, she was sure she could help even more.

"Be careful," she called out.

The creature had been facing away from him, staring at the ground and shuffling its feet ineffectually. It turned at her words, let out a piteous moan and began shuffling toward him.

"Thanks," Isaac said, throwing her a wink. "No more helping the bad guy, okay?"

Angela bit her lip, nodded. She watched him come up on the zombie fearlessly, sinking the blade deep into its shoulder. The thing collapsed in a heap on the ground, the blade coming free as it fell.

"You have to cut off its head," Angela reminded him.

Isaac nodded, swinging again. The monster's rusted red eyes came open, and flashed hunger or anger at him; they closed as the blade bit again. A few more well-placed hacks, and its head rolled free.

They fell upon the garden. There had been rations in the shelter; but they had been rations. They fed their bodies while leaving their souls hungering for something more. Isaac ate spinach leaves while she bit into a tomato like it was an apple, then they switched places. He peeled an ear of corn while chewing, bit into it and handed it to her. They spoke to each other between bites, like two best friends at closing time.

"Oh, this is so good," she breathed.

"Mmm-hmm," Isaac nodded, swallowed. "You're like, the best gardener ever."

"Awww," she said. "And you're the best husband ever. Here, have some of this kale. The bitterness really offsets the sweet of the corn nicely. Oh, sorry, there's blood on that piece. Here."

Isaac took a bite, nodded enthusiastically.

"Oh, yeah," he said around the food. "That is so good."

There was more remaining than there had appeared to be; over a week left untended was a week left unharvested, and the passersby had only taken what was visible. They spent the next twenty minutes picking and eating, until they sighed and sat on the soft soil together.

"I think that was the best meal I've ever had," Isaac noted.

"Me, too," she nodded. "We should harvest what more we can, so we can get moving."

"Get moving?" Isaac paled. "Sweetheart, I was thinking we could harvest what we could, go in the house and get some decent swords, and hunker down again. The bomb shelter…"

"Has a ventilation system that is no longer working," Angela finished for him. "All the power has failed, as far as I can tell. We tried everything to get the generator back up, but there wasn't much fuel left anyway. We can't sit still,

Isaac. We need to find out what state the world is in, and help if we can. The last news reports said that the number of howlers wasn't getting any higher; maybe they are dying off for some reason. Maybe they have found some kind of treatment."

He shook his head.

"And maybe everyone is dead," he said quietly. "Are we ready to find that? What if everyone is gone?"

"They're not," she said confidently. "We're not. We can't be the only ones. Even if we are, we can find somewhere better to live than a dark hole with no power or ventilation. If everyone is gone, then we can live anywhere."

Isaac nodded. "Alright. I'll go down and get what we need. You keep picking. They don't like the sunlight, so we should travel by day and look for somewhere safe to hole up for the night. Any particular direction you're thinking of heading?"

"Yeah," Angela turned, bent and started picking the tomatoes that were just starting to turn. "The city."

"What?" Isaac frowned. "Why?"

Angela glanced over her shoulder at him, mirrored his frown.

"The museums," she said, as though he should have known. "We need to see what people are doing with the art. We can't lose that."

Isaac took a breath, opened his mouth to speak. He closed it, forced his frown into a smile.

"Okay," he said. "The city it is. I'll get our gear."

Chapter 10

The ship was the size of a small city, bigger than their drifting island by half. Its steel hull towered over them, and blocked out the sun as it drew slowly closer. Christina stood on the sandy shore, guiding the behemoth with hand signals and calm calls over still water. A man leaned over the railing above her, hand cupped to his ear. She could barely hear her instructions being relayed, a ghostly echo that sounded every time she shouted. When the ship took up the bulk of her view, she held up a firm fist. She called out, one last time.

"That's it!" she cried. "Any closer than that and you'll get caught in the nets when you drop anchor!"

The echo was brief, a single word shouted over the sounds of sea and engine. "Hold!"

Another word followed, as the man leaned over the railing and saw her thumbs-up.

"Clear!" he called.

Chains rattled, anchors splashed loudly into the water, and her whole world was the side of the ship and the steady clacking sound for the next minute. A slab of steel slid aside a few feet above the water, and another head looked out of the hole. The unfamiliar face smiled, and she waved. The simple friendly gesture brought tears to Christina's eyes; up until a few minutes ago, she had been contemplating the possibility that they were the only ones left. Seeing a strange and friendly face released a tension in her that she didn't realize she had been holding onto.

Christina smiled, waved back. She watched the tender as it was slowly lowered past the woman and into the water. There were a half dozen others waiting by the time it smacked the surface, and they piled on to cross the open expanse of calm waves between them. She was glad to see Jason approaching along the sand. He reached her before they beached the boat, and nodded toward them.

"At least they're human," he noted.

She nodded, smiled as they approached. The first one to reach her was the one that had been leaning over the side, listening to her. He had his hand extended long before she could shake it, and was talking as soon as he stopped.

"You're Christina McMullen, aren't you?" he asked. She nodded, shook his hand. He glanced over his shoulder, called out.

"I told you so!" he said. "This is the only fully self-sufficient seastead in the world, you guys!"

"Better than self-sufficient," Jason amended, taking the man's hand when he proffered it. "I'm Jason."

"David. Nice to meet you." He turned, beckoned to another man coming up behind him. "This here is our captain, Bruce. He belongs to an ancient order dedicated to the preservation of humanity. They have ships, and a place for everyone to go, and everything!"

David sounded like a damned soul talking about Heaven; it was clear he had never been there.

"Everything?" Christina asked. She shook the captain's hand. "Does that mean you have the cure?"

"We do," the captain nodded. "We also have an inoculation, to make sure this doesn't happen again."

"Really?" Christina glanced at Jason. "Do you have any with you?"

"Pills, yeah." Bruce shrugged. "Not the inoculation, though; that's just been developed. Everyone is being treated as they enter the facility, but we haven't been back yet. We're almost full, then we head back."

"How do you keep in touch?" she asked. "How are your engines still running?"

"Same as you, I suspect." He looked past her, at the lighted windows in the houses beyond. "We had protective cages for most of our essential gear, in case of electromagnetic pulse attack."

"So that's what it was?"

He nodded. "So far as we can tell. Funny thing, though. It seemed to be selective, to some degree. Many government facilities had pulse protection to rival our own, and they went down. We found several submarines, civilian and military, that had similar protection. They were affected as well. Nothing more than floating graveyards, all of them."

Christina frowned. "All we did was line all of our generator sheds with thin mesh wiring, and our vehicle storage shed. There's not much there, a few golf carts and a couple of tractors. They all work, though. Nearly all the televisions are shot, but most of us didn't watch much TV in the first place. We didn't really lose a lot, just enough to figure it must have been a pulse."

Cocking her head slightly to the side, she went on.

"Captain," she continued, "I get the impression you aren't here to give us pills. You don't even have the inoculation. We don't need any fuel or food, and I suspect you don't either. Exactly what is it that you are hoping we can do for you?"

"Bruce," he suggested quietly, smiling disarmingly. "Please, call me Bruce."

"Alright, Bruce," she shrugged. "What is it you are hoping we can do for you?"

He smiled again. "Honestly, we are hoping to team up with you. We have a lot of resources, but we are down to a single facility. The elder members of the order asked me to come to you, and see if you would consider establishing your island as a second sanctuary. We need another place to send people, and bring people to. If anything happens to our final facility..."

Christina waited, to make sure that his trailing off was indeed a dramatic trailing off. She answered, kindly enough.

"First of all, Bruce," she said. "This is not my island. This is their island."

She turned, and included the scores of people on the beach with a wave of her hand.

"Second of all," she added, "this is not really an island. It's a seastead. It's designed to drift. As soon as it sits still, it begins to take on water. That's fine for awhile; but after an extended period it will start to sink, and will not be able to move and discharge the water it has taken on. The island can't sit still, and then take on a bunch of extra weight. There's no telling how long it would last."

Bruce let his friendly smile fall, squinted his eyes at her.

"I don't believe you," he said. "Something tells me you know exactly how long it would take for it to sink, and that it's a lot longer than you're letting on."

Jason balled up his fists, and edged forward; Christina reached out, took his hand. She whispered sweet somethings to him in her mind, felt his fingers relax in hers.

"If we let this island drift," she explained, "it will continue to exist indefinitely with minimal upkeep and maintenance. Without that upkeep, it will still provide fresh food and water for thousands of people for at least three hundred years. Those are not my estimates; they are what the independent studies showed when researchers came on the island. It's a big part of what got us our sovereign nation status. It's all based on the island drifting, though; if you make it sit still, it will sink in a hundred fifty years. Less with added load."

Bruce shrugged. "We could pump out the water, attach flotation to the underside of the island."

"What factory will build the pumps?" she asked. "What will the flotation be made of? Will it stop fish from being caught in our nets, or nutrients from rising into the soil?"

"I'm sure we can come up with something." He shrugged again.

Christina pointed at his ship.

"Did you build that vessel?" she asked.

Bruce shook his head, and she gestured at the people behind her once more. Many of them had stopped exchanging hugs and handshakes, and started listening.

"We built this island," Christina stated simply. "We have everything we need to maintain it indefinitely. There is no new technology needed to modify it; we can house and feed thousands. But we must be able to drift to do that. You're proposing that we anchor down the island with devices that don't exist, built in workshops that have turned to shrapnel, with workers that have been dead for days. I'm proposing that we let this island serve the purpose it was created for, and allow it to continue to drift. We would be happy to help out everyone not bent on sinking our island, I would wager."

Several faces that she knew were nodding, gathering closer as she spoke. Even the unfamiliar faces were nodding, and one called out his agreement. A smattered chorus of echoes followed, and Christina held the captain's eyes until the voices died down.

The captain nodded, cast a worrisome glance at the others.

"I'm quite sure I have not explained myself properly," he said quietly. "If you would meet with some of the elders of the order, I'm certain that you would come to agree with them."

Christina sighed.

"Do they want to sink the island as well?" she asked.

"Of course not," he rushed in. "No one wants to sink your island. We just want to work with you, in the interests of humanity. For the greater good."

"Okay." Christina felt her shoulders relax a bit. "It sounded a little like you wanted me to hand over everything to your 'the order', and come to work for them."

Bruce shook his head fervently.

"Not at all," he objected, in the most friendly tone he had taken so far. "That is not the order speaking, that is my perspective coming through. My apologies. I have known nothing else my whole life. For me, and the many families that I know, there is no higher service than dedicating oneself to the order. You have only just heard of us, and I did a poor job creating a first impression. I'm afraid my zeal for our cause has put you off. Again, I apologize."

Several of the onlookers were nodding again, and Christina felt herself relax even further.

"Very well," she said, smiling slightly. "Apology accepted."

"My instructions were to offer you aid," Bruce went on, "not try to enlist your help. I see you have the basics, as we suspected you would. Do you need anything else? Sundries, fuel, weapons?"

Christina lifted an eyebrow. "You have weapons?"

"Of course," he answered. "We wouldn't have made it here without them. Very few howlers want to come in peacefully, and submit to being locked up and treated. If you don't kill them, they will try to eat you. We came onto your island unarmed, as a gesture of good faith. It is the only time anyone who can handle a weapon has not had one at hand since boarding."

"I appreciate that," Christina said. "We could definitely use some weapons. We were not prepared for an actual zombie attack, after all. Our best defense is being on the water."

"You know they have gills, right?" Bruce let the information sink in, watched her smile fall before he spoke again.

"When did you last raise your nets?" he asked.

A woman spoke from the crowd that had gathered.

"Last week," she said. "Before…"

Bruce nodded. "Take your weapons when you raise your nets. There's bound to be some howlers caught up in there."

Christina shuddered.

"Thank you," she breathed. "What can you spare?"

"We'll give you everything we can," he responded. "We'll leave some pills with you, too. It won't be much, but you are welcome to follow us. We'll be headed back to the facility after this, to drop folks off and pick up more supplies."

"We can move pretty fast with the right current," she said. "But we can't cut a path across the ocean like a ship. We would only slow you down."

He shrugged. "We'll wait."

"No," Christina glanced at Jason. "We'll give you our predicted path, and stick to it. That's the best we can do."

"It's more than enough," Bruce smiled. "I will bring some of the elders to meet with you, and an ample supply of the inoculation. If you wish."

"Of course," she replied. "Meanwhile, you folks can stay here tonight. We have plenty of room, and many of us would like to see a new face and ask some questions. Everyone who would like to stay on the island, let us know. We'll find a comfortable place for you."

"What if we want to stay for good?"

The question took her by surprise. She turned to the assemblage, spoke in the general direction the voice had come from.

"It would have to be put to a vote, like we always do," Christina said. "Generally we search for people that we need, but these are obviously special circumstances. Also, if anyone that lives here wants to go…I realize that things are different now. This facility they're going to may be the best hope for humanity, and I would not begrudge anyone the desire to leave. If anyone you love is still alive, it sounds like that's where they'll end up. They may already be there. Think it over, tonight."

She turned her attention back to the captain.

"In the meantime, Bruce," she smiled. "About those weapons…"

Chapter 11

∞

Lauren set her tray on the table, settled on the bench. She turned, caught the look of surprise on his face.

"Hey, Nick," she said. "Can I buy you lunch?"

"Lauren!" He reached out, as if to embrace her. Stopping short, he patted one of her shoulders awkwardly. "Where have you been? This place is great. And lunch is free, you know that."

"I do," she nodded. "Pretty good, too. How do you like it here?"

"It's great," he said again. "It's amazing how many people lived here before. It must have been hard to dedicate yourselves to the service of humanity when humanity didn't even know about you."

"Not really." Lauren stabbed a fat bite of broccoli, held the fork before her eyes. "We knew this day would come. It always does, eventually. We have to stay vigilant, and well prepared. It's actually a very meaningful existence."

She popped the bite in her mouth, chewed while he nodded his agreement.

"So this is where you grew up, then?" he asked.

Lauren swallowed.

"Oh, no," she shook her head. "That place was destroyed, while I was out on my first mission. This is an entirely different facility. The same, but different. It doesn't matter, really. I'll be on rescue missions the rest of my life."

"Oh." Nick fiddled with the food on his plate, pushing it around disinterestedly with his fork. "Of course. I don't suppose you need a first mate for those missions."

Lauren nudged him, stabbed another sliced vegetable.

"You're needed here," she said. "You should help these people, and make this place stronger for being here. Maybe find somebody, start a family."

She said the last quietly, and bit the food off the end of her fork. Nick glanced at her; she was focused intently on the simple fare piled on her plate, or appeared to be.

"Is Allen going back out with you?" he asked.

Lauren nodded. "It seems that most or all of what he said about the zombies is true. If people are not pretty far into treatment when they get here, the hive mind can see where we are. Allen says he is the only one left that can not change back completely. It seems to be true, and we can't inoculate him until all traces of the change are gone."

"I saw him today," Nick said. "He looked totally human to me."

"Yeah, I know," she nodded again. "There's a stubborn patch of flesh on his belly, though, that looks as monstrous as his face did a few days ago. It won't go away, even with the new treatment. So he's going with me, to defend against howlers in emergency situations."

"By becoming a howler again," Nick ventured.

"Yeah," she said, "by becoming the same howler that saved us before. He wants to get away from this place, and stay away. It's very unselfish of him, offering to help."

Nick pushed away his plate.

"I suppose it's selfish for me to offer my help," he mused. "Sorry for making you turn me down. Good luck out there, Lauren."

He stood, picked up his tray and walked away. Lauren stared after him, furrowing her brow and thinking of something to call out after him. Before she could, someone else sat down.

"Hello Lauren," she said, glancing at her tray. "You need to eat."

"Yes, ma'am." Lauren chose another chunk of fresh vegetable, stabbed it with her fork. "I know. There are people out there relying on me."

She chewed slowly, listening to the woman speak.

"That's right," she said. "I wanted to visit with you before you leave again, make sure you know why we are doing what we're doing."

Lauren swallowed, nodded.

"I know what I'm supposed to do," she responded. "I am supposed to tell everyone that even this facility was destroyed, and that we have to start over together on a small island. I have the coordinates for the island, and enough fuel and weapons to continue my rescue missions for some time. Should anyone get suspicious of my occasional supply trips, there is a cache stored on a nearby shore. I can take the suspicious party or parties there, to show them where the fuel and weapons have been coming from. Under no circumstance am I to return here with any more rescues. Nor am I to encourage anything but the most basic living situations on the island; the only technology allowed is my ship, and it is to be docked far from any human habitation."

"Very good," the woman nodded. "Do you know why?"

"No, Elder Kingston," she shrugged. "I don't need to, specifically. All I need to know is that my orders are to be done in the service of humanity. I know all of you are seeing this problem from the same place, and are better able to see and understand solutions than I might. I'm just a captain, ma'am. I'm no admiral."

The woman smiled, gestured at Lauren's plate. She took another bite, dutifully, chewed it while the elder spoke.

"You brought in a very curious ally," she said. "Our new friend Allen has some very interesting things to say about what triggered this event. He's convinced that the hive mind can see more than others of its kind now. He says that they are hunting technology like they hunted flesh, and destroying it as violently. He is further convinced that we are vulnerable to this hunt, even in our hidden location. The use of technology will draw the howlers here, and they will find their way in, according to his theory. Once they have toppled the cities they will root out the last vestiges of yesterday's society and destroy them as well. That means us."

The fresh delicious flavor had gone tasteless in her mouth.

"Ma'am?" Lauren asked. "Could that be true?"

She nodded, solemn. "I believe it could. The council is divided on the matter, which is why our rescues will be divided on the matter as well. Half of our rescues will come to you, the other half will come here. We will live with our existing technology, and attempt to develop more. You will eschew technology in every way. The people on the island should be encouraged to focus on the present, and resist talking about the way things used to be. This should be a deliberate practice as the next generation is raised. The mistakes of our past must be erased for humankind to move forward."

"You sound pretty convinced, ma'am," Lauren pointed out. "Are you staying here?"

She sighed. "I am. There is to be an age limit on the island, as more children are born there. I would be sent back eventually anyways."

"Back here?" Lauren asked; she nodded. "Don't you expect to die here if you stay?"

She smiled calmly, put her hand on Lauren's. "I always

expected to die here, dear. This way we have twice the opportunity, collectively."

"Wasn't there another possibility?" Lauren pressed. "Everyone was talking when I got here, about a floating island built by people. Is that true?"

"It appears to be," the elder responded. "Some council members are on their way there, to talk to the people that built the island. Some of us are headed elsewhere, to tend to other situations."

"Other situations?" Lauren was curious. "Like what?"

She shook her head. "The less you know, the better your chances of survival. The more quickly you get on with living, the less fettered you will be by humanity's past."

"Elder Kingston," Lauren ventured carefully, respectfully, "you don't think this place will be here by the time I come back, do you?"

"Honestly, Lauren," she confided, glancing about before finishing, "I don't expect this place to be here when I get back."

Lauren fiddled with the food left on her plate. She hoped the elder wouldn't push her to eat any more; she had lost her appetite.

She glanced at the woman. "Is it okay if I talk to him about what led you to think this way?"

"Allen?" She nodded. "Of course. I expect it. He carries a great burden, similar to our own. There is no reason for him to be helping us, or telling us so much, unless his intentions are aligned with our own."

"Unless he's trying to divide and conquer," Lauren pointed out. "Which is surely the fear of the other council members."

The elder smiled. "It is. We have been conditioned to save humanity, not to trust them."

"Ma'am?" Lauren knew that word was the equivalent

to cursing here. "Conditioned?"

"Oh, yes," she laughed quietly, had another look around. "Programmed, conditioned, brainwashed…call it what you will. There is no one doing it better than us."

She paused, let her smile fall, and added, "Particularly now."

Lauren pushed her tray away, stared at her elder. It was rude to get up and leave, even disrespectful; but this was blasphemy. She was torn. The elder saw it on her face, and laughed again.

"I apologize, dear," she murmured. "I forget that you never lived outside. You're the oldest young person I know; it's easy to forget what you never got to learn."

"Ma'am?" Lauren let the confusion continue to show on her face. "Is there something I should know?"

She hesitated, had another look around before taking a good long look at the giant common clock on the industrial gray wall.

"Elder Kingston," she said quietly. "Please."

She nodded, resolved.

"We volunteers," she began, "we come back here with a different attitude, some of us."

Lauren nodded, and she went on.

"We learn out there in the world what we don't see here," she continued. "When some people are selfish in the right way, great things happen for a lot of people. When others are selfless in the wrong way, it causes great harm to many people. You would have surely learned this when you sojourned. Now you never will. That world is gone. The principle remains, but it is not what we learn here. Out there is where we used to learn the truth of our selfless missions here. We would learn that the most selfish thing we could do was come back here, and repeat the mantras, and live secretly for ourselves."

Now Lauren looked around, making sure no one could hear her.

"I could be anything out there," she said. "Or I could have been, back before all this. How could it be selfish to turn your back on endless possibilities to come back and rededicate yourself to this? I've never understood that, on the rare occasion that I've heard it."

The older woman nodded.

"You would have," she said, "after two years out there. Those endless possibilities are there for a lot of others as well; they're trying and failing every day out there. We don't see that in here. Every story that makes its way into our books and onto our screens is a success story. Out there, you realize that most folks are lucky to simply get by. Two years is exactly right. It's not enough time to really make a mark, or learn some outsider skill that will make you somehow invaluable to that world. The whole time you know that you can leave it all behind, and go back to the family you know. We all have a place here, we all have a vital purpose that we serve. Out there we become nobodies. It's a jarring adjustment."

Lauren nodded. "I always kind of longed for that. Anonymity. Meeting new people, knowing I might never see them again or be called on to save them because it was my duty. I always wondered what it would be like, to just live."

The elder reached out, took her hand; Lauren curled her fingers around the comforting feel of her papery flesh.

"I almost didn't come back, you know," she said, winking at Lauren. "There was this beautiful little town in Spain, that seemed to soothe my soul like no other place."

Lauren grinned, opened her mouth to press the older woman for details. She had never had such an intimate moment with an elder. A loud alarm sounded before she could speak, and they both turned their heads to the sound. Lauren felt the comforting grip slip from her hand.

"Yellow alert," a calm female voice came over the speaker system. "Activity detected. Armed units assemble. Outbound units expedite or abort immediately. Repeat. Yellow Alert. Activity detected…"

They turned to each other, tuned out the endless repetitions.

"That's us," Elder Kingston said. "Best of luck, Captain."

Lauren nodded. "Best of luck, ma'am."

She stood up, helped the older woman to her feet. The elder surprised Lauren, embracing her as she rose.

"Do something selfish," she whispered in her ear. "You're the kind of person that helps the world when you do."

Lauren was biting her lip as she pulled away. She hesitated, letting her troubled thoughts cloud her countenance, until the other woman laughed.

"Whatever you're thinking of, dear," she said, still laughing. "Do it."

Lauren turned, ran away without excusing herself. As casual as she had been earlier, the meeting had not been by accident. She had accessed video feeds and inbound reports that should have been of no interest to her just to have lunch with him one last time. Lauren had felt guilty for the transgressions, until the elder's words had hit home for her.

She found him at the nearest ready station for fighters. He was arguing with another man, smaller than him by a head and dressed in fatigues.

"I can help!" Nick cried. "Arm me and let me help. I've dealt with these things before. I've killed these things before."

"That's all well and good, sir," the other man said dismissively. "You have not trained with us, however. Rules are very strict on this. You must undergo our training to fight with any of our units."

"I'm a trained soldier, for God's sake," Nick sputtered. "Why won't anyone let me help?"

"Sir, I"m happy to talk about this when this mission is over," the man said, clapping another armed man dressed in fatigues on the back as he presented. "I'm sure you'll make a fine addition to-"

Lauren moved up behind Nick.

"First Mate," she said sternly.

Nick spun on his heel, grinned down at her and saluted her smartly.

"Captain," he said.

"Your ship is about to leave without you," she told him.

Lauren leaned to the side, to see around him.

"Carry on," she told the other man. He nodded, turned to fall into hurried conversation with the other gathered soldiers.

"Let's go," she said, pivoting and walking away. She didn't want Nick to see her smile, although his was still clearly in evidence. She walked quickly, comforted by the sound of his heavy footsteps behind her.

Chapter 12

The entirety of the island was ringed by a steep rise of mountain range. Only a few uprisings were less than sheer, and those places were home to the three outposts guarding the island. Two were for defensive purposes only; cannon snouts poked out of holes in the outposts, pointing outward. There were narrow slits along the walls, wide enough to put a large rifle through; the rest of the structures were impenetrable steel. Only human hands could key the doors open, and only those hands whose imprints were saved in the security database. The outposts could be overwhelmed, theoretically; each of them was equipped to be destroyed from within, in the unlikely event that they were overwhelmed. Explosives were set to take out any invaders present, and make the pass impassable.

The third break in the mountains was the largest by far. It was the only way in or out, and none passed through the entrance without giving up something. They waited in line, listening to the repetitive drone of the voice over the loudspeakers. Many were starving, and nearly everyone was thirsty; some were wounded, and having trouble standing. Every break in the line was investigated immediately by unsmiling men with pistols at their belts and riot masks over their faces. At one end of the line, people were being processed at the rate of one per ten to fifteen minutes. The messages over the loudspeaker were repeated nearly a dozen times before the line would inch forward with each successive processing.

"Attention to all civilians," the impersonal voice blared. "This is a survivor processing facility. Part of this processing will determine if you are fit to live among the community that we on the island call home. There are very strict rules to joining this community, and no one will be forced to follow those rules. They are a prerequisite to joining the community, however. Please listen closely. If any of the following conditions are not to your liking, let your processing agent know when your turn comes. If these are acceptable terms, we will work with you to make sure you are placed properly within the community. Everyone has a job here, and is committed to the common good of everyone else. Please memorize the following."

There was a pause in the recording before the rules were stated; it seemed increasingly deliberate each time it looped around, although it remained the same length. Even more deliberate was the music that rose behind the voice as it went on. It was a tinny and vague mishmash of a dozen national anthems, and it played as monotonously as the voice that spoke over it. People shifted uncomfortably through both sections; nearly everyone stirred during that pause. Many people's eyes went glassy when the music started, and some began to silently mouth the words along with the recording.

"This city is founded on basic principles, and a set of rules comes with those principles," it said. "There is to be no talk of your life before this place. There is to be no attempt at creating new technology, or smuggling in old technology. This island is meant to take humankind back to its fundamentals, and forget together what nearly caused its demise. No member of this community is permitted to speak of zombies, or history, or technology; we must leave these thoughts behind if we are to begin anew. This will be a new age, 'The Age of the Innocent', and this will be our Eden. Any transgressions will result in immediate and permanent banishment of all individuals involved. We are glad to have you, once you accept these terms. While you wait, let me tell you about our home."

The music got louder, at this point. It also got more mathematically chaotic than impassioned, although that was clearly what the composer had been going for. The voice went on, more jaunty and upbeat, occasionally drowned out by crashing cymbals and blasting horns.

"Welcome to the outer reaches of Eden," it continued. "There is plenty of food and water for everyone inside, and enough room for all of the surviving members of humanity to live comfortably. Quarters have been arranged, and they will be assigned according to the work you are given. The island is well protected, and there is no need for any new residents to bring weapons into the inner garden and living area. Furthermore, all technological devices are to be shed before processing can occur. You will see bins lining the hallway; put anything that is not natural in those bins. If it will not fit, set it near the bin. Stay clothed, but understand that those materials will be removed as a part of processing. Any jewelry or accoutrements not made by hand must be deposited in the bins. Handmade items will be inspected on a case by case basis, and may be selected for disposal by your processor."

The voice went on to tell them what a fine selection of food awaited them, and how close the cafeteria was to the processing station. It told them to expect inoculations, and immediate assignment to a work unit. It told them that there were hundreds of people inside, and thousands more coming. It told them that this was the only place that they were of aware of for folks to go, but that those not wanting to follow the rules would be deposited on a nearby coastline and left to fend for themselves. It told them that there were no guarantees of their safety anywhere but here, and that howlers still roamed the Earth in numbers far greater than people. It told them that their only hope was to give up their past, relinquish their belongings, and swear their obedience to silence.

One by one, in ten to fifteen minute increments, that's what nearly every one of them did. By the time the last person in line was processed, another ship had arrived; the line grew long once more, and the loop continued its patterned indoctrination. The ship stocked up on fuel and supplies, boarded those that turned away the ideas of the island, and took them out to sea. The crew fed the lot of them a feast generously seasoned with sea salt, ground pepper and cyanide.

When they were all dead, Bruce personally chopped off their heads and tossed the bodies over the side of the ship.

Chapter 13

∞

"Do you hear that?" Angela stopped walking, cocked her head to the side. She turned to Isaac. "It sounds like gunfire."

He stopped as well, listened.

"It does," he said. "That's a good sign, right? Doesn't that mean people? We haven't seen any other zombies; maybe the military bounced back, and is containing them."

Angela shook her head, started walking again.

"The buildings are still being destroyed," she said. "That's why we're not seeing them. They're inside, burrowing into foundations like rats and toppling all the skyscrapers. Look at the skyline. This is not the city we once knew."

Isaac nodded. "So it could be humans fighting humans."

"Yeah," Angela said, "and we only have swords. Be careful."

They kept walking, and the sounds grew closer.

"It's coming from the museum," Angela said. "It's still there."

Her pace began to pick up, and Isaac glanced worriedly her way.

"Oh, no," she said, her breathing coming faster. "What if they are trying to destroy the art? Isaac, what if people are defending the museum against zombie attacks? Come on!"

She was running suddenly, and he had no choice but to keep up. He saw the building at the same time as she did, and they skidded to a stop together.

"Look!" she cried. "They're trying to get in! We have to help!"

The wide entrance was packed with bodies in various stages of living or dying or dead. There were dozens of howlers, blocking the doors they had flung open, fighting each other and the waves of bullets that pelted them. Some fell, only to rise again; others fell, and did not get up. The remaining monsters tossed them aside, or began eating them. Gunfire erupted continuously from the other side of the door, and the creatures were being driven back by the interminable assault.

"Sir!" A voice called out behind them. "Ma'am, be careful!"

They turned together at the the sound; a man in jeans and teeshirt approached them, an automatic rifle cradled awkwardly in his arms.

"Hi, folks," he said. "Sorry for startling you. You were about to cross the line of fire."

He pointed, and they saw others. Two men and a woman were approaching the invading monsters from behind, rifles at the ready. They signaled to each other, then to him, still moving forward. The man signaled back, and nodded.

"Got to go," he said. "Stay here."

Angela saw a spare clip tucked into each of the back pockets of his jeans. One was working its way out with every step the man took, more metal showing with each long stride. She stepped forward, to call out to him; Isaac took her hand, pulled her back to his side. He shook his head, and put a shushing finger to his lips; they watched silently as the clip slipped free. It clattered loudly to the pavement, and the others gunners turned to the sound. Their attention was on him, and the howlers that started at the sound were only visible from Angela's perspective. By the time she called out, one of the monsters was halfway to the group where they were coming together. Two more trailed behind it.

"Look out!" Angela ran toward them, watching the group burst apart as the first monster reached them. Two were hit, and went flying; the other two backed away rapidly, firing at the creature at will. Angela knelt beside the man who had welcomed them where he lay in the street. A wide gash had opened his torso like a zippered coat, and his entrails were cascading out over his legs.

"Did it bite me?" he gasped. The man tried to sit up, causing a fresh wave of thick blood to wash over the pavement. Angela shook her head; she held his shoulder firmly, pressed him back to a lying position. Doffing her jacket, she doubled it over and lifted his head with one hand. With the soft bundle slid under his head, she let it drop slowly onto the cushion. She glanced at his face, and frowned.

The man's eyes were lifeless, staring.

Angela reached for the rifle, threw the strap over her shoulder. She picked up the spare clip where it had fallen, leaving the other to drown in the growing puddle of the man's blood.

"What are you doing?" Isaac asked, standing over her.

Angela rose, planting her feet firmly so as not to slip in the slick wet stain. She glanced at him, then at the gun in her hands.

She shrugged. "I'm going to help."

The two perimeter guards that still remained were backed up to a vehicle that had been abandoned some time ago. It was a newer panel van, made to look old by the ravaging effects of the apocalypse. The tires were all flat, the windows shattered and dangling shards of glass;

even the paint looked pitted and worn, beyond anything a good wash and wax could polish up. The side panel door had a sizable dent in it, and they cowered together in the concavity. Each of them slowly emptied their clips in bursts, as the other reloaded. Step by agonizing step, the last howler was coming at them. Bullets tore through its chest and face and legs, and every few strides it would fall to its knees; it got back up each time, and came for them again.

Angela ran at the monster, calling out to it.

"Hey!" she cried. "How about a face full of this?"

She stopped, leveled the rifle and pulled the trigger. The weapon jumped wildly in her arms, and the spray went wide. Planting her feet more firmly, Angela brought the butt of the weapon up to her shoulder. The next spray of bullets caught the creature as it dipped to all fours to come at her; it's face was whipped about by the volley, and one of its eyes exploded in a burst of blood. The zombie fell forward, and lay there unmoving.

"Nice shooting." The man and woman that had been backed up to the van came towards them, him nodding as he spoke. He glanced at the museum entrance, then at the woman walking with him. "Can you help us clear the last of them?"

Angela followed his glance, saw a few monsters clawing their way over a mountain of corpses. She nodded, held the rifle sideways for him to see.

"Yeah," she said. "If you'll show me how to change the clip."

Chapter 14

Allen was staring at the rations like they had already been eaten once and vomited back onto his plate. Lauren glanced at his meal; there were no bugs or distasteful goo, only bland rations that looked much like what filled her tray. She took a bite, forced herself to chew, and glanced at Nick. He was almost finished, plowing through the flavorlessness like it was top shelf sustenance. In a way, it was; in every other way, it was totally unappealing. Lauren took another bite, nodded at Allen's portions.

"You should eat," she said. "You need to stay healthy."

Allen laughed darkly.

"I'll never be healthy again," he muttered. Nonetheless, he scooped up a forkful and put it in his mouth. He chewed, his features screwed up in disgust. Lauren nodded, and took another bite of her own. Allen was still chewing when she swallowed, his face still twisted.

"You need to stay strong." Nick finished his plate, nodded his agreement. "We may need your help again."

Allen kept chewing, kept his eyes on his plate. After another minute had passed, he paused to swallow. The movement looked painful, and unfamiliar. His eyes found each of them before they dropped to his plate again.

"The only way I can be helpful is by dying, or killing," he muttered. "The only way I can stay strong is to eat people. If I do eat flesh, they may know where we are. If I don't eat it, they're apt to find us anyway. Then we're defenseless."

"Not really," Nick shrugged. "You can just eat them when they show up, and take pills and go back to a regular diet each time they aren't around. You can transform completely by eating one of them, right?"

Allen pushed away his plate.

"One or two of them, I'd say." He met Nick's eyes, and his frown deepened. "And what do you expect them to do while I eat them? Just lay there?"

"Of course not," Lauren cut in. "We kill the first few, and fight the rest off while you feed. I kind of thought that was the plan."

Allen shook his head. "Do you know how hard the transformation is? Not just physically, but…well, in every way. I have to live with the things I've done for the rest of my life; it's not just a mask I can pull off and put back on. I become a monster in my thoughts too; there's about as much left of me in my howler mind as in my monster face."

"I still recognize you," Lauren shrugged.

Nick shrugged as well.

"I'll do it," he said.

"Do what?" Allen leveled his gaze at him.

"I'll let one of them bite me," he said. "I'll turn each time they show up, and turn back when they aren't around or when they aren't attacking. I didn't get inoculated."

Lauren threw him a sharp glance.

"You didn't?" she demanded. "Why would you do that, Nick?"

"It's not tested," he shrugged. "It could have adverse effects."

Allen chuckled darkly.

"It could render men impotent, or women infertile," he mused. "That would be a grand irony, wouldn't it? The medicine designed to prevent another violent apocalypse causes a slow sighing extinction instead?"

"That's awful," Lauren frowned. "Whose side are you on, anyway?"

Allen lifted his shirt, to show her.

"I am forever on the fence," he said. "Which is why I should be the one to do what you need. If I need an ally, I'll come find you and bite you, buddy."

He grinned at Nick, without a hint of humor. He dropped his shirt back into place, in time with Lauren pushing away her plate.

"Bite me first," she said, seriously. "I didn't get the shot either."

Nick laughed. "Hypocrite. Why not?"

"Lots of reasons," she shrugged. "Same as you."

The device at her hip buzzed; Lauren palmed it, held it before her on the table. She shook her head while she swiped through screens, and darkened it before addressing them.

"We're approaching a ship," she said. "It looks like a cruise liner, knocked out by the pulse. Is everyone done here?"

Nick stood, while Allen gave his tray of rations one last baleful glare.

"It's amazing, you know," he said quietly.

Lauren paused, her hand on the door. She glanced at Nick, and he shrugged. Turning, she let her hand fall to her side. They watched him remember, together.

"There's no guilt, no shame," Allen went on quietly. "They say that howlers are as smart as people, but it could be argued that they're even smarter. There's no lack of focus, no hierarchy of needs to be met before a person can think clearly. There's only hunger, and a mind bent on fulfilling it. If animals feel that way, they live in bliss. And when they kill, it's fucking transcendental. Feeding on flesh changes you, and even those that change back will never be the same."

He glanced at Lauren.

"You know," he said.

Nick straightened, and looked at her. Caught between the two penetrating sets of eyes, Lauren lifted her hand to the doorknob once more.

"If you're coming," she said, "then come on."

She walked out, and heard them trailing behind her. Nick's hurried footsteps caught up before she reached the next door.

"Is that true?" he asked. "Have you…turned?"

"Yeah," she said brusquely. "I have. He's right. It is the most terrible wonderful experience I've ever had. Not that I've experienced much."

Lauren yanked the next door open, strode through it, and called back over her shoulder.

"I'm only sixteen, after all," she said.

Her next steps took Lauren to the planking that lined the foredeck. She approached the railing, looked up at the other ship. When she heard them approaching, she began to cry out orders to the other passengers they had taken on.

"All gunners report to Nick," she called out. "Lower the tender, and drop the ladder for me."

Lauren glanced at the tight knot of people surrounding Nick already. She smiled, slightly, and glanced at Allen.

"You coming?" she asked.

Chapter 15

Angela had torn her own clothes to pieces, bandaging the wounded. Her jacket and buttoned shirt were in strips, holding in lifeblood on half a dozen arms or legs. She was down to an undershirt and shorts that had been jeans before she'd started tearing pieces off them. Isaac was tying the last bandage tight, knelt next to a stranger beside her, when the man opened his eyes and grasped Isaac's arm. Rather than draw back, Isaac leaned in. He smiled as best as he could at the man; Isaac had seen his wounds.

"Just relax," he said soothingly. "Lie back."

"You," the man gasped, trying to use muscles that had been sliced to uselessness. He was looking at Angela, even as he fell back. "I know you."

Angela shook her head. "I don't think so, friend. I'm pretty good with faces."

He smiled. It looked like it pained him to do so.

"You don't know me," he said. "But I know you, Ms. Chrysler."

"Oh?" Angela's brow furrowed, and she checked his dressings one last time.

"Your books, honey," Isaac smiled.

"Oh!" she looked at the other man, and he nodded.

"You need to save it," he said. "You need to save all of it."

Her eyes rose to take in the walls around them. They

were bare, outlines showing where pieces had hung over the years. She shook her head.

"It's all gone," Angela said. "And you'll be fine."

The man laughed, spit up a bit of blood, and shook his head.

"No, I won't," he said. "I know that. We've been collecting all the art we could, from all around the city. It's not gone; we have brought it all to upper or lower floors that we can defend. These folks need a leader, and a planner. You need to save everything you can."

"What about the capital?" Angela glanced at Isaac, back at the other man. "What about the books?"

Isaac cocked an eyebrow, shrugged. The man gasped, and nodded.

"Angela Chrysler," he breathed. "Save it all. You have to."

She nodded, fervently. "Of course. Of course we do."

He chuckled one last time, and closed his eyes forever.

Several of the others had been watching. They came forward now, to lift the corpse onto a stretcher. Angela bit her lip, glanced at Isaac again.

"What are you doing?" she asked them, moving aside.

The woman that looked at her held her eyes for a long moment. There was a depth to her stare that conveyed a sadness Angela could only imagine. The woman looked hungry, and tired, like the others. There was something else under the hunger and fatigue, and it did not look like hope. Angela looked away, watched them carry him out.

"We're going to cut off his head," the woman said flatly. "Then we're going to burn his body, so he doesn't come back."

Angela shuddered. "I'm so sorry."

"He lived longer than most folks got to," the woman mused, moving away with one of the handles to the stretcher clutched between both hands. Angela turned to Isaac, her eyes going wide.

"We need to finish what he started," she insisted. "We need to save it all, like he said."

Isaac saw the light in her eyes, thought of the dullness he had seen in the gaze of the other woman. He took her in his arms, pulled her close to him. Angela's arms wound around his shoulders, and her lips brushed his ear.

"We can do this," she whispered, and he nodded. Isaac had seen her put her mind to something enough times to know that it would not easily turn from a meaningful task.

"Let's go outside with them," she said, pulling away slowly. "Let's mourn their dead with them, and mourn ours too. Then let's save all of the best that humankind has had to offer. The next generation won't be lost if they have the arts to draw from as they rebuild."

Isaac turned, moved toward the exit with her.

"Rebuild?" He laughed darkly. "The world isn't done falling apart yet. Who's rebuilding?"

Angela took his hand, began to lead him more quickly toward the wide entrance.

"We are," she said, over her shoulder.

Chapter 16

Nick sat across the table from Lauren, and tried not to watch her eat. Her motions were mechanical, almost obligatory; Lauren's thoughts were clearly elsewhere. He was no more interested in the rations than she was; Nick was here to talk, to take advantage of the rare opportunity when it presented itself. He pushed the food around his plate, cut large chunks into chewable pieces, but did not take a bite. Instead, he spoke.

"Captain," he said, "We seem to be following a different action plan on this rescue trip. Are we targeting certain areas, or being rerouted? The system has totally changed."

Lauren nodded her agreement, continued her distracted chewing. When she swallowed, and took another bite, Nick went on.

"It's strange to have to keep Allen in a cell, too," he said. "He's not taking the pills so he can help; it's torture for him to starve and then feast, and to live in a cage when he's not killing."

This time she swallowed, placed her fork carefully on the table, and answered him.

"He volunteered," she said. "The confinement is for his own safety, and to keep the passengers calm. Nearly everyone on board is in shock, Nick; if an armed person sees a howler, even if he has a friendly name tag, they are too likely to shoot first and ask questions later. It's how most of these people made it this far. I would rather have him caged than killed, and Allen himself agrees."

Lauren sighed, picked up her fork again. Pushing pieces of processed flavorlessness around on her plate, she frowned at the food. She set her fork down once more, turned her frown on him.

"I am not privy to the order's plans," she said. "But I do know some things. I know that there are three active rescue ships remaining, ours and two others. I know that we are not to share itineraries with each other. I also know that they saw mine. So I found a way to read theirs."

Lauren's eyes went glassy, as they had so often lately. Her gaze fell to the table between them, and she sighed once more.

"Captain." Nick pushed his plate away. "What's going on? What did they say?"

Shaking her head, as if to negate what she had seen somehow, Lauren answered nonetheless.

"One ship," she said, her voice trembling slightly, "is gathering people of accomplishment. They're rounding up artists, engineers, celebrities, journalists and authors, and skilled workers that demonstrated great drive in the old world. They're taking half of them to some island, the half that agree to their rules, to build a new technological center for the world."

Lauren paused, bit her lip to keep it from trembling; it didn't work.

Nick put aside the title, to breathe her name.

"Lauren," he said. "What about the others?"

Now her voice did break, and Nick couldn't blame her.

"They're killing them," she cried. "If they don't sign on for whatever plan the order is putting into place, they are taken off the island on the pretense of returning them to the world. A few miles out to sea, they chop off their heads and toss the bodies in the ocean."

The blood drained from Nick's face, and what little he had eaten tried to come up on him.

"That's insane," he said. "There are so few of us left."

"The other ship," Lauren went on, quietly, "has the same orders that we do, up to a point. They are to systematically scour the ocean in sections, and bring all survivors back to Eden."

Nick shuddered.

"I'm sorry, Captain," he said, "But I hate that place. The constant droning recording, the long lines of ragged survivors barely keeping their feet. I tried to give one of them a bottle of water, and security stepped in right away. They told me not to have any further contact with anyone but administration, and told me to get off the reception floor immediately. It's hard to believe that everyone is agreeing to their conditions, even if there is the promise of food attached. What happens to the others?"

"They leave," she said. "On the other ship. A few miles out to sea…"

Lauren trailed off, and Nick shook his head as he felt his face pale further. They both looked at the table between them, and the uneaten food, lost in their own thoughts. After a minute Lauren spoke, her voice a quiet shadow of its usual self.

"That's why we're following such a strange path," she said. "We're trying to find the people that they're going to kill before they do, and give them a place to go."

"Where?" Nick asked. "There's nowhere left."

"There is one place," she said. "It's built to last; some would say it's built just for this type of occasion. It's close to the coast, and is ready to be engineered organically to be a fertile valley again. Even though it's right under their noses, the order won't go there; it's considered to be a sacred place by them, in the worst way possible. They would sooner destroy it than visit it, but that is forbidden as well. It's perfect."

Nick furrowed his brow, shook his head.

"What do you mean?" he said. "Egypt? The pyramids?"

Lauren nodded. "One of them is gone, the Great Pyramid. We'll rebuild it. We'll bring together all the best minds and workers we can, and build a testament to humanity that will also serve as a warning to generations to come. We'll start over without the need to start over, and we'll jump humanity ahead instead of forcing it to fall behind."

"No one knows how the pyramids were even built," Nick said.

"The order does," Lauren said. "I do."

His eyebrows shot up, and he leaned forward out of genuine curiosity; another thought struck him then, and Nick frowned.

"Have you talked to Allen about this?" he asked suddenly.

The question hung in the air for so long that he didn't think she was going to answer. Lauren even glanced at her abandoned meal, and moved her hand toward her forgotten fork on the table. Her hand went still before it reached the utensil, and she sighed again before answering.

"I have," she said. "It's sort of his idea."

Nick took a deep breath, tried to make his voice as calm and casual as possible. Lauren noticed right away, cut him off.

"Allen sure has some strange ideas-" he began.

"You don't trust him," Lauren said. "I know. I'm not sure I do either. I do think it might be worth listening to his 'strange ideas' before dismissing them. The order has many beliefs that are in line with what he is saying. Hell, it's built around them. I thought I was going to go crazy, once I realized how the rest of the world lived. There was no impending prophecy of doom hanging over their heads, no constant preparation for the day when people started turning to monsters. I had a moment of doubt, and I wondered for years after if the order was just a bunch of crazy people."

Lauren broke off, held his eyes for a moment and then looked away. She went on, her voice whispered sadness.

"My greatest fear," she said, "was that I would go out into the world and not be able to cope, that I would have to return because the crazy had soaked in. My greatest fear should have been that they were right. It should have been that their horrible prediction would come true. It should have been that the zombies would come before my freedom did, and that my lack of faith would be my greatest shame. I betrayed them, not believing; now I am betraying them again, not trusting in their plans."

"Lauren," Nick's voice was as soft as hers, and as quiet. "You are doing the right thing. They're killing people. We have to stop them, or at least save as many people as we can."

"You were in the navy, weren't you?" she asked.

Lauren's voice was her own again, strong and confident.

Nick nodded. "I was."

"You killed people." She stated it simply, and he nodded again.

"I did," he said. "I signed up to stop people from doing what the order is doing right now. I learned to kill people to save those who couldn't save themselves. I never killed anyone that was not armed, or in charge of people that were. I certainly never killed someone because they were too smart, or too accomplished, or too well-known."

Lauren's eyes had gone cold, and Nick wondered what

mantra was spinning through her head as she replied.

"What if they do know better?" she said. "What if they're right, and the only way to save the world is to choose who survives to rebuild?"

Nick leaned forward, tried to find her somewhere in her eyes.

"What if they don't know better?" he asked. "What if they are using this as a chance to take over what little is left of the world, and shape it their own way? There's a big difference between remembering history and foretelling the future."

Lauren looked away before he could see her, exhaled impatiently.

"You don't understand, Nick," she said. "They know things. They've always known things. The order has watched humanity rise and fall dozens of times; it's always the same. Two cultures begin anew, one a culture of enlightened technology and the other a group starting from scratch."

"Always?" Nick interjected. "Is it natural, or do they engineer it? And what exactly is 'enlightened technology'?"

She shook her head, still wouldn't look at him.

"Enlightened means non-violent," Lauren said. "That culture always falls, eventually. Someone always weaponizes something, and they are wiped out. It's how it has to happen, though; the books all say so. One day a technological society will rise that is peaceful, and humankind won't be starting from scratch. One day the fall will be followed by a new rise, a version of humanity like none before. The Earth will look upon them, and she will be pleased. She will not destroy them."

"Lauren." Nick leaned forward, searched her averted countenance. He reached across the table, to take her hand; she moved it away.

"Please," he said. "You have to consider that the order

is the reason this cycle keeps being repeated the same way. They are probably the ones that wipe out the technological culture when it first conceives of weapons. There is no way of knowing if the next step is a peaceful one if the order interferes before they can take it. Can't you see that they're engineering history to repeat itself?"

"It has to," Lauren breathed. "It always does. The order doesn't cause it; the spirit of the Earth does."

It was Nick's turn to withdraw. He pulled his hand away, dropped it in his lap. His eyes found the floor.

"Allen believes me," Lauren said. Her voice was strident, stark. "He's seen the Earth Mother. He calls her Maya. He says she took human form, to send zombies across the world, and then destroyed her human form. He says she caused the pulse, that it was her final act before going back to spirit form."

Nick searched the floor now, without hope.

"And still," he murmured, "you trust him."

"He met her," Lauren said.

Her voice was beginning to rise, and she stared a challenge across the table at him. Nick did not lift his eyes. He only shrugged, to say that what she offered as proof struck him as proof of something entirely different.

"And you trust him." It wasn't a question, and Nick did not await a response. He stood, met her eyes at last.

"You trust a zombie," he said, "who claims to have met the spirit of the earth in human form. Didn't he also say that he betrayed and murdered the woman he loved? How do you know he won't betray you? How do you know that he isn't planning to murder us all, by learning where everyone is gathering and helping you decide where the rest should go? How do you know you're not acting against one evil to set up the dominoes for another?"

His hand was on the door when she called out; he

stopped at the sound of her voice, listened.

"Nick, please," she said. "I have to trust someone."

Turning just enough to catch her eye at last, Nick frowned.

"Maybe you do," he muttered. "Clearly it isn't me."

Chapter 17

Christina stood on the beach, watching the ocean span across the horizon. Most of the island residents were lined up behind her, their eyes locked on the same stretch of sea. Her face was calm, and clear; the residents muttered doubtfully among themselves, and shifted uneasily as one every few breaths. None of them raised their voice to her, and Christina was silent until Jason came to stand beside her.

She glanced at him, smiled, and put her eyes back on the horizon.

"Any luck?" she asked.

"If you'd call it that." Jason squinted into the dying sunlight. "We got an old radar working, and we saw what the message said we would see. There are three ships approaching, all pretty good sized."

He spoke low, aware of nearby residents leaning in to hear. Christina took his hand, squeezed it and let go. She turned her back to the horizon, and faced the people lined along the shore. Some of the faces were new; most of them she had known for years, many of them decades. Behind those faces were minds that she had marveled at, and worked closely with. As Jason turned his back to the ocean, she swept her hand to include as many of them in the gesture as possible.

"They need to know," she said. "You tell them, or I will."

Jason nodded. He cleared his throat, eyed the sea of wondering faces. A few caught his eye, and he smiled sadly at each of them before he began to speak. Jason raised his voice that they all might hear.

"You're right." He frowned, glanced over his shoulder. "These are our friends, our family. Even the newcomers are finding ways to contribute already. We got this far with trust, perhaps it will take us even further."

The residents crowded closer, the newcomers beaming at being included while they sensed dark words ahead. Jason went on.

"As many of you know," he said, "we received a morse code message this morning. What most of you don't know is exactly what the message said. It repeated over and over for several minutes. When we tried to respond, there was no reply. The message was simple. It said, 'Three warships coming. They will take the island. They will kill McMullen.'"

Christina shuddered at the words, was glad she hadn't been the one to speak them. She glanced at Jason, nodded. He continued.

"We got an old analog radar working," Jason said. "There are three ships coming. They will be visible on the horizon within the hour, unless they slow their course to come in under the cloak of darkness. Either way, we have reason to believe that the warning may be real now that we know they're coming. I'm not willing to take the chance. We're leaving. Anyone who wants to come with, meet us at the docks in thirty minutes."

"Jason!" A man lurched forward, pushing others aside. "What else did the message say? Are they going to kill the rest of us?"

Jason grasped her hand, pulled Christina a step closer to the water.

"I don't know," he said. "Everything I know, I told you."

He turned, still grasping her hand, and started walking toward their home. Christina looked back over her shoulder, several times, but kept pace.

"Where are we going, Jason?" She searched his face, saw only grim determination.

"Away from here," he frowned. "Somewhere safe."

"It's not safe anywhere," she said, still walking. "We seem to live on a zombie-free island. There were none in the nets when we pulled them up. As long as we burn our dead right away, this island might be our best bet."

"Not if they're coming for you." Jason kept pulling, and she kept following. The beach had disappeared over the shallow rise of the soil, and she had stopped looking back. "Not if they want to kill you."

They walked in silence to their house, brisk and grim. When they were inside, he smiled and let her hand go.

"Get everything you need," he said. "We might not be coming back."

Christina frowned, looked all around her.

"I need our home," she said. "I need this island. This is everything great I ever accomplished. I can't leave it."

"Your books," Jason said quietly, gently. "What about your books? You changed lives with the things you wrote, with the books you published. Grab copies of all of them. As many as I can carry. Wherever we're going, we'll need them."

Tears began to form in her eyes, and Christina blinked them back before they could fall. She nodded, moved into him, wound her arms about his waist.

"Okay," she said, into his shoulder. "Okay. We'll leave."

She was finished before he was, with less luggage. Jason shook his head as he came up the hall, frowned at the small pile.

"Get everything," he said. "I can manage. I'll go grab the cart trailer from the garage. I can pull that fully loaded, no problem. You go get what you need, everything you need."

Jason threw open the front door, froze, then began laughing. Christina stopped at the sound, turned in her tracks.

"What?" she said. "What's so funny?"

"Grab whatever you need, Christina!" A voice echoed Jason's sentiments, from the other side of the door. "We're here to help!"

A few steps and she saw them, fifty or so people waiting to lend a hand. Jason grabbed suitcases immediately, turned them over to the nearest person. He stepped away, to be replaced immediately by another set of outstretched hands. Jason smiled, stepped inside to grab more bags. As he turned them over, the man leaned in and spoke softly.

"You might want to hurry," he said.

He waited until he saw that it had sunk in, spoke again as Jason nodded.

"We saw them," he said. "Soon as the sun dipped down, they crested the horizon. They're running dark, and coming in fast. No way we would have seen them if we weren't watching. I think you're making the right choice."

He watched Jason nod again, took up the bags and turned away. He called back over his shoulder as a woman took his place on the porch.

"They're coming fast," he cried. "You might want to hurry."

Chapter 18

With all three bottles filled and stuffed, Joe lined them neatly on the counter. He checked the rags once more, pausing to coax one a little further into the bottle. Setting the lighter on the counter beside them, he sighed and glanced at his wife.

"You can change your mind," he said, quietly.

Shawna shook her head.

"I can put this gas back in the generator," he continued. "It will give a us little more light and heat when we need it."

"We're out of food," Shawna replied, in low quiet tones of her own. "We picked the garden clean, before we couldn't go downstairs anymore. I know you don't want to do it, but you're the one who pointed out that we have no choice. If we wait any longer, we won't have the strength to fight or travel. It's him or us, like you said before."

Joe frowned.

"He might still go away," he said. "Or we might get our hands on some of those pills we heard about, and help him…"

Shawna took his hand, smiled soothingly.

"We can't get anything in here," she said. "No food, no pills, nothing but shelter. Besides, they have to want to take the pills. That howler has been waiting around in our yard for three days now. He's not out there trying to locate the cure; he's out there because he wants to eat us."

Joe nodded, glanced worriedly at the bottles.

"It's him or us," Shawna said again.

Joe nodded, more confident.

"If this doesn't work-" he began.

"Then at least we tried," Shawna finished, resolutely.

Squeezing his hand once more, Shawna let go and reached for the lighter. She moved to the window, pushed the curtain aside.

"He's just laying there," she whispered, still looking out the window. "He looks smaller than before."

"He hasn't eaten in days," Joe said. "Let's hope that works in our favor as well as brick walls and steel doors and staying on the second floor have so far."

"Do you want me to come down the stairs with you?" Shawna stepped closer. "I could hold the bottles, light them for you…"

Joe shook his head.

"Watch from the window," he said quietly. "And barricade the door behind me."

He didn't hear the dresser slide back into place after the door closed behind him, and Joe nearly waited for the sound. When it didn't come, he stepped up one stair. The bottles shifted in his arms, and he moved against the wall to keep them from slipping. Once he had righted them, and himself, Joe sighed and moved slowly down the stairwell. The sound still didn't come.

At the lower landing, he set the bottles near the wall and flicked the lighter a few times. Each time, the flame leapt immediately to life; satisfied, Joe slipped the lighter in his pocket to lift the heavy barricade from the door. Two television wall mounts had made for sturdy supports; the four by twelve board had been part of his heavy desktop back when civilization was still somewhat civilized.

Joe removed the board, as quietly as possible, and set it

aside. As he reached for the bottles, the door creaked open at the top of the landing. Shawna's whispered warning floated down the stairs.

"I think he heard you," she said. "He's moving around, looking like he might get up."

"Thanks," Joe muttered, digging the lighter out of his pocket. "Close the door, Shawna. Barricade it."

She nodded, clicked the door quietly closed.

The dresser did not slide back into place, so far as he could tell.

Kneeling next to the bottles, Joe found his fingers wanting to fumble at the spinning wheel that suddenly didn't want to spin. He took a deep breath, bit his lip and tried again.

The flame leapt to life, startling him.

Joe touched the tip to the rag, lifting the bottle and standing as he did. He glanced at the peephole, but thought better of looking out. The lock clicked and turned easily, and Joe grasped the knob to swing the door open wide. He stepped back, his arm cocked behind him, and threw the first bottle just as he glimpsed the monster.

It was loping toward him, with the sure slow swiftness of a crazed killer, before the door even opened. When the bottle crashed at its feet, it skidded in its tracks to slide into the flames. It howled as its hands caught fire, as the flame licked at its face, and again as the next flaming bottle took it square in the chest.

For all the flames, it may have been hard to tell who or what was burning for a moment. The monster turned slow fiery circles in the drive, its voice silent while dark smoke trailed from his flaming form to fill the sky. Then it stopped turning, howled, and began walking toward Joe once more.

His hands were somehow much steadier than he expected them to be as Joe touched the flame to the last rag. It went up with a whooshing sound, and the monster hesitated for the briefest of moments. It dropped to all fours suddenly, dashing forward just as Joe threw the last bottle. It had been aimed at the creature's feet, to engulf it in flames all the more completely; when the howler leaned forward and moved, the bottle struck the concrete and his face simultaneously. The burst of flame and glass found its way into the monster's mouth, around the back of his head, and slowly met up with the flame that already burned on the howler's shoulders.

Joe watched it writhe for a few moments, then watched it lay still at last. The smell of burning gasoline and flesh hit him all at once, and his stomach turned upside down all of a sudden.

Closing the door, Joe didn't bother with the heavy board. He trudged up the stairs, stopping halfway as the door flew open above him. Shawna stepped to the landing, a wide smile lighting her face.

"You did it!" she cried, happily.

Standing half on one step and half on another, Joe nodded. His eyes found the stairwell, then her. He nodded, once more, numbly.

"I don't think I can do it again," he said.

Shawna's smile fell, and she descended the few steps between them to rest a hand on his shoulder.

"You won't have to," she assured him. "We'll find food, we'll find others like us, we'll find a safe place to go."

Joe nodded, moved his head to brush his lips against her hand.

Shawna smiled. "You're my hero, Mister Compton."

He kissed her hand again, lingering longer. Finally, he smiled.

"I love you, Missus Compton," Joe said.

Chapter 19

The voices were right on the other side of the door, making no effort at all to be quiet. Doug tried to ignore them and go over his material at the same time. The exchange was making it difficult.

"I think we should eat the comedian," one gnarled voice said.

"That's Doug Benson, man," the other voice came back.

It was as twisted and monstrous as the first voice, but Doug brightened at the words. He was the only human on the ship, after all; he needed to take any ally he could get.

"I know who he is," the first monstrous voice spoke again. "I still think we should eat him."

"And how would that go?" came the response. "How many bites would you get before the others jumped in to tear him apart? How long before his flesh started to taste zombified, and was no different than us starting to eat each other? We're the last civilized group of howlers, the earth mother's final organized strike. We can't eat the comedian; he's a symbol of our discipline."

The first speaker was uncomfortably quick in responding.

"We could find a new symbol," he said. "One that doesn't smell like food, and twist my gut with hunger every time he walks by. Let's just go in there, you and me, and eat the guy. No one needs to know."

"We share a mind with the others," the other spat. "How stupid are you, man?"

The moaned reply barely reached Doug's ears through the thin door.

"I'm no man," he said. "I'm a howler. A very hungry howler. We were not made for discipline; we were made to feast. Hell, even you smell like food to me now."

A fresh chill climbed Doug's spine, getting lost in a series of them. He reached for his phone, reflexively, and remembered it was no longer even able to tell him the time. Doug dropped his hand, leaning in to listen, wondering if it was time for him to go on yet, wondering if anyone would be coming to look for him.

"I don't like the way you're talking," Doug's monstrous champion said through the door. "You need to come with me, have a little talk with the lieutena-"

The sentence ended with a thump, and another that sounded against the door. Doug jumped back involuntarily, started digging in his other pocket while they scuffled loudly on the other side of the door. Each time a body thumped loudly against the thin barrier, it shuddered and bowed inward for a frightening moment.

Doug found what he was looking for, put it between his lips, and lit it. He took a long smooth pull, held the smoke in for a short second, and let it stream out in a cloud that obscured the door for a moment. The scuffling stopped after a minute, and Doug smoked the joint as calmly as he could while he waited to discover if he was to be rescued or eaten.

The door opened, and one of them stood in the frame. It eyed him, while blood dripped from its mouth to puddle on the floor between them. Wiping it with the back of a camouflaged sleeve, the monster smiled a toothy grin at him. It was not enough to indicate whether it was his champion or the other, with all those bloody teeth glinting in the green room light. Then the creature spoke, and Doug sighed smoke at its words.

"Mister Benson," it said. "I think we need to get you out of here. I am beginning to fear for your safety."

"Yeah," Doug nodded enthusiastically. "You and me both."

"I'm Howard," the monster said. "I'm a big fan."

"Well, alright. Good to meet you, Howard." Doug leaned into the door frame, cast a cautious glance each way before continuing.

"What's the plan here?" Doug whispered, taking one last long hit.

"Follow me." Howard turned, began moving away from the doorway. "Stay close, keep quiet, and listen even more closely. There is importance in everything I say."

Doug moved out of the smoky space, dropping the smoking roach and stepping on it in passing. It wasn't something he would have ordinarily done so off-handedly, but it was hardly a mess next to the remains of the fellow that had wanted to eat him.

"Does this mean no more post-apocalyptic comedy shows?" Doug mused quietly. "Thank God. I was running low on zombie jokes."

Howard halted so abruptly that Doug nearly ran into the monster as he turned. His rusted red eyes were intense as they burned their hungry gaze into Doug's.

"They can see through my eyes if they want," Howard whispered fiercely. "They need to see me taking you on a tour, where nothing I say means anything, until they can't stop us. But everything I say means something. May we resume the tour, Mister Benson?"

"Yeah." Doug nodded, sobered by the searing outburst. "Got it."

They moved swiftly, until they were on deck under the bright sunlight. Doug shielded his eyes, looking around.

"Where are all of them?" he asked.

"Sleeping, most of them," Howard responded quietly, moving toward the railing. "The sunlight is not harmful to us, but we do our best work at night. There's a security crew, posted in those lookouts…"

Howard pointed a taloned finger one way, another, then a third.

"…but they're probably sleeping too."

At the railing, Howard pointed again.

"Security has gotten more lax the last few days," he continued. "There are explosive charges out on deck, directly above the fuel tanks. A rocket of virtually any size fired anywhere around either would sink the ship almost for certain."

Howard pointed once more.

"See that submarine?" He waited until Doug nodded before going on. "It's fuel cells are in the rear of the ship, where plastique is being shaped to place on other ships as we find them. After we eat whoever is aboard, of course."

"Of course," Doug breathed.

Howard met Doug's eyes again, nodded.

"Let's continue this tour below deck," he said.

Doug followed the monster. As they descended what began to feel like an interminable set of stairs, Howard spoke over his shoulder in a hushed and hoarse whisper.

"We are the last organized group of…"

Howard hesitated, his feet moving while his sentence stalled. Finally, he spoke the word. His head was down, and the word almost too quiet for Doug to hear.

"Zombies," Howard breathed. "We're the last organized group of zombies. We're systematically scouring the world for survivors, and eating them. The other zombies are eating each other, all across the world, as mother nature intended. They will all die soon, and humanity will have another chance to rise. Unless we succeed, that is. On this ship, we are forbidden from eating each other. Our captain is obsessed with wiping out everyone. The whole crew shares his obsession."

Following behind Howard, Doug was not able to see the creature's face as he spoke. He frowned at Howard's last pronouncement, as they kept moving.

"It doesn't sound like you do," Doug pointed out.

Howard threw a glance over his shoulder, and met Doug's eyes for a brief moment. Doug's breath caught in his throat, involuntarily, as the rusted red eyes seemed to glow with hunger.

"The whole crew shares his obsession," he growled.

His head whipped around again, and Doug found his breath once more. They kept descending, in silence, for a few flights. They went through a door, and another, before Howard spoke again.

"Do you know how to drive a boat?" he asked.

Doug shook his head.

"The small ones are pretty simple," Howard said, approaching another door. "Same with small submarines, there's not a whole lot to controlling one."

"Oh." Doug tried to sound interested. "Okay."

The door came open, and Doug smelled fresh ocean air as bright sunlight speared his eyes. When the world went from blurred flashbulb to lighted details, he saw what Howard was pointing at.

"There's only room for one person," Howard said, "which means all the controls are in easy reach. Just open that top hatch and…"

Howard trailed off, as Doug arched an eyebrow high.

"You want me to drive that?" he asked.

They looked at the miniature vessel together, both of them frowning.

"It's really quite simple," Howard muttered.

"For a navy guy, maybe," Doug retorted. "I'm a comedian, man. That's things not big enough for me to stretch out in."

"It's not for stretching out in," Howard growled. "It's for single soldier underwater subterfuge."

The monster turned his way, fixed Doug with his rusted red glare.

"And escaping certain death," he added.

Doug still looked at him uncertainly, and Howard sighed.

"If you can drive a car, you can skipper the stealth sub," Howard assured him. When Doug continued to glance doubtfully between the monster and the machine, Howard sighed again.

"If you can work a vaporizer-" he began.

"I get it." Doug held up his hand. "I"m just steeling myself, okay?"

After steeling himself for another half minute, Doug stepped forward. He knelt next to the mostly submerged vessel and cranked the wheel. The door opened with a quiet sigh, and swung easily outward. He peered inside.

"Do you see the controls?" Howard's voice came behind him.

Doug nodded, but didn't glance back.

"There are just two controller sticks," he called back.

"Yep, easy," Howard said. "Like a video game. Do you see the one with the trigger on it?"

Doug nodded, gulped at a sudden lump that decided to form in his throat. Rather than speak past it, he turned this time. He nodded again.

"That's for the rockets," Howard said. "Drive with one

hand, shoot with the other."

They held each other's gaze, both of them frowning.

"I can't," Doug said at last.

"You have to," Howard growled.

"What if I miss?"

"The same thing that will happen if you don't try at all," Howard shrugged. "They will hunt you down, and destroy or eat you."

"Alright," Doug said. "I'm going, then. Wish me luck."

As he settled into the narrow seat and got his bearings as best he could, Doug chuckled. There was more than a little nervous tremble to his voice when he spoke again.

"Here I thought you were saving me," Doug said.

Howard laughed out loud; it was a monstrous sound, one that Doug had grown accustomed to hearing. Those howling peals of terror had kept him alive these last few weeks or days or however long he had been a zombie pirate ship comedian.

The monster's laughter gave way to a sad and somber look.

"You're saving humanity," he said, "as long as enough others do their part to save it too. Most of all, though, you're saving me. Godspeed, Doug Benson. The sooner you pull that trigger, the quicker you save my soul."

Howard turned, as bloody tears welled in his rusted red eyes. He went through the door in the hull, closed it behind him without looking back, and left Doug with the miniature death machine.

It was easy, just like Howard had said it would be. The controls and smooth flowing underwater movement in three dimensions made it seem even more like a video game, and the strange rise and fall of the ocean currents contributed an almost psychedelic element to the experience. Doug found himself holding his breath, in the exciting unreality.

Then the vessel drifted, and its light speared through the water to show him the broad side of the other submarine. It was a very large and very daunting reminder of reality for him.

Doug breathed, took a controller in each hand, and rested his index finger on the single trigger. A low tone filled the close cabin, rising in pitch as the vessel continued to drift. When the giant sub filled the entire view port, red light flooded the cabin and the tone rose in both pitch and volume. Doug's eyes went round, and he squeezed the trigger.

At first he thought that a shark had swum past at incredible speed, headed in the direction of the other submarine. Then he realized, as he watched it, that it was a small torpedo. Doug held his breath again, watched the swimming trail of bubbles behind the rocket as it made a strangely swift and slow path through the water to the hull of the submerged behemoth. The closer it got, the smaller it seemed, and the submarine seemed as though it should be no more concerned than a man watching a fly come in for a dramatic landing on his shoulder.

As it neared, Doug felt certain that it would bounce off or sputter out just short of its destination. The howlers would drag his little vessel back in and eat him while he was still full of fear and false hope. He thought it must all be an elaborate prank, Howard serving Doug up with some heart palpitations before serving Doug up to the crew.

The rocket struck the side of the sub, and exploded. Doug saw nothing but flashes of light and endless bubbles as his little vessel was rocked backward from the explosion. A second followed, almost immediately, and Doug resisted being thrown about the cabin while trying to steer away from the heat and light. The vessel's light speared into darkness, and Doug followed the light full speed. He dove until a third rumble filled the water and seeped sound into the cabin.

This was not a single explosion, but a series of them. Controlled and rhythmic, Doug knew that sound. It was the giant warship's engines firing up, like they did every evening as the sun went down. The sun was still high in the sky, however; and Doug knew there was only one human they were hunting now.

Turning the little vessel, he saw the submerged hull of the ship hove into view. Doug sighed, rested his finger on the trigger once more, and held his breath as the low tone filled the cabin again. The tone grew louder, and more high-pitched, as he pushed the little vessel forward. Long after the red light came on, flooding the cabin with light and illuminating his face with an eerie glow, Doug pressed forward. He swung alongside the ship, angling along it until the giant spinning propellors came into view.

Doug squeezed the trigger.

This time the torpedo didn't startle him; he watched its lazy rapid path of bubbles until he knew it was on target, then squeezed the trigger again.

Another torpedo tore through the water, headed in the right direction.

Doug squeezed again.

As a third rocket moved toward the slowly trundling ship, the first struck. It exploded with such concussive force that Doug could see it, and could watch the other torpedoes dip and churn as the wave hit them. They continued on course, approximately, and another struck the damaged hull higher toward the water line a moment later. Doug squeezed the trigger again, but nothing happened. The red light and whining electronic cry had both been extinguished, and Doug was pretty sure he was out of torpedoes.

Before the third could strike, and rip another hole in the thick metal, an enormous explosion bent the hull outward in a half dozen jagged pieces. The water turned to fire, the last missile dwarfed by the ship's explosives catching alight. Fragments of ship and hull and monsters that used to be people shot out in all directions.

Doug's little vessel turned end over end in the flaming waters, drifting aimlessly deeper into the water and further from the ship.

Doug sagged at the controls, unconscious.

Chapter 20

∞

Lauren put the binoculars to her eyes, biting her lip as she scanned the horizon. Nick stood behind her, eyeing Allen as the monster shared her view. It was always cold relief when Allen had to feed to ensure their survival. He was spending more time on deck during his long recovery periods, and more and more passengers were sticking to their quarters. Nick couldn't blame them; if it weren't for his sense of duty, and his loyalty to his mission, he would be far away by now.

When she spoke, it startled him. Nick was so lost in his thoughts that he jumped slightly at the soft sound of her voice, and his hand went to his holster. His eyes had gone to Allen, and it was strange to watch the monstrous man gaze at him with such disdain. His lack of concern seemed to be tempting Nick, taunting him with the knowledge that the monster was the man in this situation.

Lauren didn't notice, any of it.

"It's not just one boat," she said, still looking through the dual telescopes. "It's four, no five. At least six."

She let the binoculars fall to her side, glanced at them each in turn.

"It has to be them," she said. "The direction they're coming from."

"Who else has six working vessels of any size? Either it's them or it's the order," Allen noted, unperturbed.

"And what do we have to worry about, either way? If they were zombies I would know. I'm still deep enough to be connected."

"If that's true," Nick said, "shouldn't you go below deck? If it is them, we don't want to freak them out. If you're the first thing they see out on deck…"

"Nick," Lauren spoke more forcefully.

"No, he's right," Allen nodded, drifted back from the railing. "They should have me explained before they meet me. Anyone deserves that."

"I'll take him down," Nick said, following Allen's drift.

Lauren frowned.

"He can find his own way," she said.

"He can't lock himself in," Nick countered, "and the others are all afraid to. He can't get to his flesh supply, either. I should feed him, shouldn't I?"

"Nick," Lauren repeated sharply. "Don't talk like that. Like he's an animal."

Nick threw another glance over his shoulder before following Allen belowdeck.

"He's not a man either, Lauren," he said, almost too quiet for her to hear.

She was left alone on deck with her binoculars and her confusion. Lauren sighed, letting herself wonder how the ship could be full and seem empty all at the same time. It was several minutes before Nick rejoined her, quietly crossing the deck to stand silently behind her.

"They're almost here," she said, to hear her own voice.

Nick nodded, looking silently past her at the approaching marine caravan. He could see people on deck now, they were so close. They weren't moving to the railing, or waving hello; the people held back even as their vessels drew near. Lauren glanced at him, but Nick kept his eyes on the strangers. She followed his gaze, moved to the railing.

"Ho there!" she called out. "Is everyone on board all right?"

The folks on the far deck exchanged glances, and a few nods. One of them stepped forward, called back.

"We're all alright!"

"Are you…" Lauren trailed off, began again.

"Is Christina McMullen with you?" she cried out.

Nick threw her a strange look, finally, but still said nothing.

A woman came out from one of the cabins, waved her hand in greeting. Nick saw Lauren's eyes go wide, and her hand clench the railing suddenly.

"Ms. McMullen," she shouted, waving with the hand that wasn't clenching the railing, "please come aboard. We have enough food and water for everyone, and we can make space."

"No, we can't," Nick muttered behind her. "We've been making space. There's no more space to make."

Lauren pointed across the water, and smiled at him crookedly.

"She'll figure it out," she said. "She'll figure it all out."

Chapter 21

The sky seemed like it had somehow gotten clearer. Rolawndo squinted against the last dying embers of the luminous sunset, sipped at his phlask, and smiled.

Maybe it was all in his mind.

He sipped again, cast a glance over his shoulder.

"Lefty!" he called out, casually.

Rolawndo rose slowly, dusting off his jeans.

"Lefty! Here, boy!"

He was gazing toward the cabin, expecting the lean wolfish form to appear from the shadows under the porch. Something had been making quite a ruckus under there a few nights ago, and Lefty hadn't been able to stay away.

A form appeared, but it wasn't the dog. Rolawndo peered into the shadows, making out what he could in the last few rays of sunlight. It was human, or appeared to be; he could swear that it looked like half of his face was missing, and that his eyes were dull and lifeless smears of rusted red. It could have been the shifting shadows, or a trick of the dying light; but that's not what it looked like. The man was moving toward him, slowly. His motions looked pained, and forced.

For some reason Rolawndo thought of the last thing his friend had said to him, after giving him directions to the secluded cabin.

"There won't be nobody for miles," Justin had said, in

his slow measured drawl. "Nobody but you and grandpa. He made us swear to bury him under the front porch. It was a royal pain in our asses, but we did it."

Rolawndo sipped calmly at the phlask, and watched the unreal staggering approach of the shadowed form. The closer it got, the lower the light got, and he shook his phlask next to his ear to check its contents.

There was plenty left. There was no reason for him to be seeing things, or be anything better than mildly buzzed. He called out, as the rambling form got closer.

"Hey, mister," he said. "You okay?"

A piteous moan escaped the mouth of the staggering form, and a chill found its way up Rolawndo's spine. The figure lurched closer, and he held up a hand.

"I think maybe you better not come closer," he said.

It kept coming, and he opened his mouth to issue a more serious warning. Movement on the beach caught his eye then, and Rolawndo turned to the streaking shadow.

"Lefty!" he called. "There you are. Come here, boy!"

It was pure primal pleasure to watch him run, even when he was but a shadow flitting among shadows. Rolawndo watched the strange lumbering form out of the corner of his eye, until Lefty veered sharply to intercept it.

"Lefty, no!" Rolawndo moved, far too slowly to stop the suddenly growling streak. He watched Lefty leap, and land fully on the chest of whoever had been approaching. They went down together, in a heap of shadows and sand and inhuman snarls. He heard Lefty yelp, followed by a thick wet sound. The other thing yelped then, and let out a strangled cry. The wet sound came again, and the cry went silent.

Rolawndo lit a match, cupped it over the trembling shadows.

"Lefty?" he asked, quietly.

He was still chewing at the man's throat, and normally

Rolawndo would have been doing all he could to save the fellow. The match threw more light on the thing's face than it did the dog, though; and it gave him a moment's pause.

Its eyes were still open, and they were a dead rusted red. Its mouth was open, too; and Rolawndo could see sharp biting teeth that were as jagged and inhuman as the sounds the thing had been making. Much of the flesh had fallen off its face, and he could see glimpses of exposed sinew in the wan light. It wasn't making any more noise, with most of its throat gone, but it was still struggling mightily. It was trying to crush Lefty in its macabre embrace, and the dog was smashed to its chest with the effort. Still Lefty bit and chewed, and Rolawndo stood there and watched.

Finally, Lefty put his powerful jaws around the creature's exposed spine, and crunched down loudly. The light in its eyes went out, and its mouth lolled with death instead of some strange sickness or hunger.

Rolawndo kicked at the head, watched it roll away from the body. He knelt, and scratched Lefty between the ears.

"Good boy," he said, frowning. "I think it's time to turn the phone back on, buddy."

Lefty yelped, and dashed toward the ocean.

"Lefty!" Rolawndo started after him, sighing heavily. "The cabin's the other way, boy!"

He saw it before Lefty hit the beach, and Rolawndo came up slowly behind the dog with his eyes on the approaching lights.

"What's it been, a week?" Rolawndo sipped at the phlask. "Two? Three? We haven't seen another soul; it's been pretty great."

Lefty barked, enthusiastic agreement.

"Now we have a visitor by land and a visitor by sea," he mused. "All in the same night."

They watched the lights grow closer, saw them stop a

hundred yards from shore. A minute later a smaller single light speared toward them, and began moving closer to them over the water.

"I'm not telling you to rip any more throats out, buddy," Rolawndo muttered. "But I'm not telling you not to either yet. Stand by."

He walked closer to the surf, capping the phlask and stowing it in his back pocket. Rolawndo called back, quietly, one last time.

"Use your best judgement," he whispered, "and hang back for now."

Rolawndo turned, called out.

"Hello!" he cried. "Who goes there!"

There had been a steady splashing sound, that was getting louder as the craft drew closer. It stopped when he called out. A moment later, a man's voice came back across the waters.

"We're human!"

Before Rolawndo could wonder why he would start with that, the voice came again.

"We're friendlies!" he called out. "We're looking for someone! Rolawndo Swells! Any way you can help us?"

"Who's doing the looking?" Rolawndo called back.

He glanced over his shoulder at Lefty, shrugged.

The man called out what sounded like the beginning of a long and drawn out explanation, and his words had trouble swimming over the waves in the exact order he had sent them out. Rolawndo squinted into the darkness, and called out to cut him off.

"Hey, man!" he shouted. "Bring her in, let's talk on shore!"

The wet rhythmic sounds started again, and he was reminded of the corpse lying on the ground somewhere between him and the rest of the bourbon. He muttered under his breath, to Lefty.

"Did you hear that, boy?" he asked. "It sounded like he said the word 'zombie' a couple times. What the fuck?"

Lefty shifted in the shadows; otherwise he stayed still.

When the boat was a dozen feet out, Rolawndo stepped into the surf and sloshed through the water to grab it by the narrow prow. He hauled it to the beach, along with the three men inside.

"Thanks," the man in front said, stepping to the shore. "I was hoping we would find you here."

Rolawndo peered at the man in the sparse moonlight.

"Do I know you?" he asked. "Is there a reason you're looking for me?"

"You don't know me," he answered. "My name is Bruce. I'm captain of that ship."

He pointed to the distant light, and then swung his hand so it hovered in front of Rolawndo. A low growl started behind him when he didn't shake it right away, and Rolawndo hushed the dog with a backward glance.

"Okay, Bruce." Rolawndo clasped the man's hand. "You found me. Now what?"

"With most of the population gone and howlers still on the prowl-" Bruce began.

Rolawndo cut him off, right away.

"Hang on," he said. "You might want to back up to the beginning. Most of the population is gone?"

He looked to the men standing behind Bruce, to see if they were eyeing the captain warily. They weren't; they nodded when he met their gaze, each of them dropping their eyes to the sand after. The end was something everyone there to see it had to remind themselves of again and again before it really sunk in. Rolawndo saw that slow sinking in that had changed these men, that had etched lines in their faces that sea madness could not carve.

Suddenly, his knees did not want to hold him. Rolawndo lowered himself to the sand, and remembered suddenly that his phlask was not quite empty. He uncapped it, and drained it.

"I need to check my phone," he muttered, putting his hand into the sand to push himself to his feet once more.

"It won't work," Bruce said, quietly. "Almost all electronic devices got fried in the pulse. Even if it didn't, the networks are all long gone."

Rolawndo lifted his hand from the sand, let it drift to Lefty's sinewy shoulders. He petted the dog calmly for a moment, letting his eyes drift from the darkened sea to the faces of the men before him. He noticed that their clothes were tattered, and some had blood on them; they were all thin, and gaunt, and they looked permanently frightened of something.

"What's a howler?" he asked, finally.

One of the men winced at the word. Bruce nodded, and answered.

"It's a type of zombie," he said.

"Oh, yeah?" Rolawndo tried to keep the disbelief from his voice; he did not completely succeed.

"Yeah," Bruce echoed, as the men behind him nodded. "The other type are slow and stupid, and they're called ramblers. They are normal folks that have been bitten, or that recently died."

Rolawndo cast a glance over his shoulder, reflexively.

"Oh," he said, quietly.

He sat for another half a minute before he spoke again, his hand drifting aimlessly while his mind calmly wrapped itself around the situation.

"Okay, then," Rolawndo said, at last. "What now, Bruce?"

"We need you," Bruce replied immediately. "There are two places where we are starting over again, and you are one of the few people who can choose which group to be part of."

Rolawndo raised an eyebrow, glanced at Lefty.

"How fortunate of me," he said evenly. "And what exactly are my choices, Captain?"

Either Bruce did not detect the change in his tone, or he didn't care. He answered in a brisk and friendly manner, while Rolawndo continued to pet Lefty.

"One group will be the center of technology for the new history," he said proudly. "You are invited to join us there, and write history as we would have it be told."

Rather than question his phrasing, or jump up and down in glee as Bruce's tone suggested he should, Rolawndo continued to pet Lefty in silence. The captain went on, after a moment.

"The other group is starting over from scratch," he said. "You are invited to join us there if you would rather, to cultivate the gardens and help feed the next wave of humanity."

He hadn't seen it at first, but Rolawndo caught a glint of steel while the other man was speaking. Glancing at the other men, as they nodded along with his exuberant invitations, Rolawndo noted that they were all armed. Not only that, they were starting to look like they wanted to reach.

His hand went still over the dog's fur, and Rolawndo smiled.

"The gardens sound good," he said. "Just let me get some of my things."

"Jordan, give the man a hand," Bruce said sternly. "We'll wait here."

One of the men stepped forward, and they walked to the cabin together. Lefty trailed them, stopping to sniff at the corpse in overalls as they passed it.

"I thought you didn't know," the man said, glancing back at the dead shadow.

"That just happened," Rolawndo shrugged. "I didn't have time to figure it out before you folks showed up."

He opened the door to the cabin, crossed the small living space to stand at the counter. Rolawndo spun the cap off the bottle, and took a long draught off the bourbon. He held it out to the man.

"Captain won't let you bring that aboard," he said.

Rolawndo held it out still, raised an eyebrow. Jordan took it, and took a swallow. He coughed as he handed it back, thanked Rolawndo with a wordless sputter.

"This place we're going," Rolawndo said. "Have you been there?"

"No." Jordan shook his head, frowned. "I saw the howlers, though. I watched the cities begin to fall. I watched everyone die. It can't be worse than that. If it is a place those things can't reach, I can't wait to get there."

Rolawndo passed him the bottle again, watched Jordan as he drank.

"If I had said no," he said, watching the beaten man's wary gaze as he handed back the bottle, "what would he have done?"

Jordan dropped his eyes, and wouldn't meet Rolawndo's again.

"Same thing he's done with all the others," he said quietly. "He would have killed you, and chopped off your head."

They drank in silence for a minute, each man lost in his own thoughts. When a shouted voice carried across the beach to find its way through the open door, Jordan started. He turned to the sound.

"Guess we better get going," Rolawndo said.

Chapter 22

When they heard that she was back, everyone came to see. Those that hadn't met her had heard the stories, and those that had knew they were true. They were the ones that had been there, and watched her fight off howlers or outrun ramblers with a canvas or sculpture clutched tightly to herself; they were the ones who had written her off a dozen times, only to watch her appear time and again with another priceless piece. They were the ones telling the stories, and the ones who had arranged the surprise.

The others couldn't help but be excited, it was so contagious. Some had even helped set up the surprise, though they hadn't met her yet. Anyone who talked to anyone about Angela seemed to want to meet her and help her almost immediately. So it was that they led her, those she knew and those she didn't, to the basement of what had once been a great museum. A dozen people spoke at once as they descended the wide stairwell, and Angela knelt every other step to come face to face with a child.

"Hello!" she sang to one. "Are you healthy? Is everything alright?"

The little girl nodded, her eyes going wide, and ran off to tell her friends that she had talked to her directly.

"Hello!" Angela knelt beside another child, for a heartbeat. "You look so happy! I'm so glad you look so happy!"

She didn't slow down or break stride, and it seemed as though she was somehow giving each person that crowded the stairwell her full attention. The children were all glowing by the time the assemblage had gathered at the bottom of the steps. Angela swept them with her gaze, and grinned widely.

"So many children!" she cried happily. "You saved so many children while I was gone!"

"You were right!" a woman called out. "There were a lot of children whose parents gave their lives to save them. They've been in upper stories of buildings, or in old bomb shelters. We've been scouring every structure that is left standing, and finding them. We're working around the clock."

Angela nodded.

"Good," she said. "Well done, Deanna. There are less buildings standing than there were when I left, and I imagine they won't stop falling until they have all fallen. We need to save as many children as we can."

She looked around, as if only now suddenly becoming aware that nearly everyone was acting like they were about to start jumping up and down like some of the children had when she had addressed them. Angela met nearly every person's gaze before she spoke again, as if silently telling each of them that they were valued and important. Her eyes lingered longest on the children.

"Now," Angela said brightly, still smiling. "What is it that you wanted to show me?"

One of the children ran to the door, and threw it open. Angela gasped at the first glimpse, and stepped back.

"You found it!" she cried. She whirled, and saw Isaac coming down the stairs behind them. "They found it!"

"It was in a vault," Deanna said, smiling. "Someone stashed it when the outbreak started, probably. We found some other pieces too."

"Don't ask how they opened the vault," Isaac grinned. "Let's have a look inside."

He stepped through the doorway, and Angela followed. Isaac grinned while she exclaimed with every new sight that captured her gaze. Canvases hung on every wall, some of the most popular pieces in history. Da Vinci paintings and sketches left little room on one wall for anything else, and the Degas and Monets took up much of the remaining space. What little was left was dominated by bookshelves, and they were carefully laden with ancient leather-bound volumes. The only wall that had been left mostly bare was above the only other furniture in the room. A wide four poster bed was in the center of the room, pushed against that wall.

The bed was directly under Van Gogh's oil rendition of a certain starry night, and Angela stopped breathing for a few timeless moments as she beheld it once more.

She breathed at last, swept the room with her eyes.

"Is this for us?" she asked, glancing at Isaac.

"It's for you," he smiled. "I will, of course, be sleeping here too."

She grinned, and threw her arms around him.

"Just for tonight," Angela murmured in his ear. "Then we have to leave, first thing. They found a boat."

"I know," Isaac muttered. "I had hoped you might not find out so fast. Alright, we leave first thing. Meanwhile, tell these people thank you."

Angela released him, beaming, and turned to the waiting group.

Chapter 23

Christina smiled as disarmingly as possible, and met Lauren's eyes across the table.

"I can't captain your ship," she said. "I'm sorry, but I won't. You've got some great plans, and I can be of help with some of them, but I won't take over your ship or your mission. Neither one is for me. I'm sorry."

Lauren was clearly crestfallen. She looked around the table for support, accustomed to the kind of meetings where people did what they were asked to do. Nick looked like he couldn't agree more, as he nodded his understanding. The two men and three women Christina had brought to the meeting were doing the same, and one had looked at Lauren the whole time she was asking like she was proposing self-immolation.

"Your order has got some pretty good resources," Christina went on. "But your ideas are not ideal, and I can't commit to carrying out those kind of plans."

"I'm not with the order anymore," Lauren protested.

More than one person looked at her disbelieving; but only one counted, and Nick was the first to cast that telling glance her way.

The others were those she had brought with her for support. Ignoring their unspoken messages, Lauren wished she had brought Allen instead.

"The order took your island," Lauren pointed out.

"They wanted to take you, too. I warned you, remember."

"Your warning could have been a little more clearly stated," Christina replied. "More people would have left if they knew the circumstances of the invasion. I'm still not clear on it, and we've been talking for nearly ten minutes."

"They took your island," Lauren said, her eyes finding a fixed spot on the table and remaining there as she spoke. "They would have come ashore armed, if I know their ways. Any resistance would have been put down immediately, and everyone who did not offer resistance would have been incarcerated until they could be processed."

"Are you serious?" The man at Christina's right exploded quietly. "Anyone who took up arms against armed invaders were put down? You mean killed, right? Say killed if you mean killed. Don't talk about our friends and family like they were animals."

Christina looked at him while he spoke, as did the others. Lauren kept her eyes on the table, and took in every word.

"My husband," Christina said, a smile dancing about the corners of her lips. "Jason. Sometimes he expresses my own thoughts with more clarity than I do, somehow."

The anger that had been in Jason's voice was not echoed in Christina's. Something else pulled Lauren's eyes from the fixed spot on the table, to see the tears that stood out in the other woman's.

"If someone had sought to take over one of the order's facilities," Christina said, "would they have encountered armed resistance?"

Lauren couldn't look away, or protest at the question.

"They have," she said. "They did."

"Your people," Christina went on, "murdered my people for doing exactly what they would have done, were their situations reversed. After having armed them."

Now, Lauren couldn't even speak. Still held by Christina's tearful gaze, she nodded.

"You understand my husband's reaction, then," Christina said. "We could have saved them, if we had known."

Lauren found her voice.

"It was a simple coded message," she protested. "I had to choose my words carefully, and keep them to a minimum."

"A few more could have made all the difference," Christina noted. "We need all the great minds we can get, to get started again. We lost a few in the invasion, for sure."

"The rest are lost, too," Lauren sighed.

Her eyes found that fixed spot again, and her voice came back stronger than before.

"I saw the plans," she went on. "Your island is to be anchored and added onto. It will sit off the coast of Africa, too far from Eden to be seen by the naked eye and close enough to watch the valley of the Nile from a safe distance. Their technology will be built there, by the people who agree to work on what they are told to work on. Any effort to make weapons for anyone who is not a member of the order's security will be punishable by death. It is meant to be an enlightened technological society, with all forward progress dedicated to non-violence."

"Unless you're a member of the order," Jason snapped.

"That's right." Lauren nodded, her eyes staying on the table. "They will be well armed, and watching us carefully from a distance. They have renamed the island by now, as well. Your seastead is now the island of Atlantis, and it's legend begins as it makes one last trip to its final destination."

"So it can slowly sink," Christina said quietly.

There was a long moment of silence, as everyone got lost in their own thoughts or each other's. Lauren kept her eyes on the table, and did not lift them even when Christina spoke again.

"Don't tell me any more about the island unless I need to know," she said. "And stop talking about these places like they are actually Eden or Atlantis. We need a practical plan, not vague predictions or even more vague recollections. Why are you so convinced that we need to gather everyone in the valley that they will be watching so closely? Why not somewhere else? Hell, why not anywhere else?"

"They will hunt you," Lauren muttered. "They will kill you. Unless you are on the move, or in the valley of the Nile. That is where everyone needs to gather, all those minds that are necessary to start over. It is the one place they won't go, even when you develop technology to prevent them from spying. Any member of the order that goes there sacrifices their life in doing so; it has always been that way, it will always be that way. It is the only place we can start over our own way, and not risk being destroyed."

"It sounds like that's exactly what they want," Christina mused. "Why would they avoid that area, for so long?"

Nick spoke for the first time, his voice raspy with exhaustion.

"They think it's cursed," he muttered. "They think the spirit of the planet lives there, and that she will kill them if they go there. I say 'she' because we happen to have someone on board who claims to have met this spirit, in human form. He claims that she caused the zombie outbreak, and that she died but didn't really die. He's a zombie, by the way. He can't turn back completely, so we keep him aboard to kill other zombies when we encounter them."

All eyes were on him, and Lauren noticed as he finished that there was a slight slur to his speech.

"Nick," she said. "Have you been drinking?"

"Lauren," he said, imitating her stern tone. "Have you

been plotting with a zombie who claims to have plotted with Mother Earth, in person, to wipe out humankind?"

He got up, and made for the door. Lauren heard him mutter something under his breath as he pulled the door shut behind him, and she thought she heard it pretty clearly.

"Of course I've been drinking," he muttered.

She met Christina's eyes, pleading silently with her.

"You've got six working boats besides this one," Christina said. "Send the four fastest vessels in each direction, plotting a course that will pick up two or three of the people on the order's list with each boat. Keep this ship moving, and set rendezvous points along that movement with the rescue ships. You find those at sea, or on islands, and save them. When you get full, send the four ships on longer missions and bring everyone that you have found to the valley. Keep one vessel nearby, for emergencies."

Lauren had lifted her eyes again, to watch the other woman as she spoke. Her mood lifted as the commanding words flowed, and she was almost smiling when Christina trailed off.

"What about the sixth boat?" she asked.

"Load it up with fuel and supplies," Christina said. "We are leaving in the morning, to set things up in the valley. I'll take any volunteers that want to go, except you."

Christina met Lauren's eyes, and shook her head.

"You captain this boat, you keep up the rescues," Christina said, her eyes still locked on Lauren's. "Find whoever is left, and bring them to me."

"Yes, ma'am." Lauren nodded.

"My name is Christina," she reminded her.

Lauren gulped.

"Yes, Christina."

"And Lauren?" Still her eyes held her, and Lauren felt her lighthearted moment passing her by.

"Yes…Christina?"

"I should meet this zombie you've been…getting advice from," Christina said. "I assume you think he's legitimate, in some way."

"I do." Lauren nodded.

"Then maybe I should hear what he has to say too."

Chapter 24

It had been hard to make friends on the voyage, which was unusual for Rolawndo. Every conversation that he tried to have derailed as soon as it veered into subjects that mattered. Where they were going was secret in all but the most general of terms, what they had been before was forbidden from being discussed, and any further probing got him nowhere but outside the ragged social circles that had formed. The crew wouldn't speak to him at all, and the captain seemed to have no interest in explaining why Rolawndo hadn't been given the same list of rules to live by as the others.

He tried not to care, sitting on the deck late at night and glad he had filled the phlask before boarding. He petted Lefty, and talked soothingly to him, and thought about the way things used to be until the others started moving about on deck in the early morning light.

Then they were there, and he was being rushed past a long line of folks waiting. A droning voice sounded overhead, and some of the bedraggled people lined up were mouthing the words in perfect lifeless time. Rolawndo felt a chill creep up his spine as some of the words came together in his ears, and then he was grabbed abruptly by the arm.

"You can't go into the garden with those clothes," a voice grunted in his ear.

Rolawndo was spun about, and found himself staring

into the eyes of a very large and very well-armed man. Two others flanked him, rifles at the ready.

Lefty growled, and a rifle shifted to train on him.

"You shoot my dog," Rolawndo said, twisting free and stepping between the barrel and its target, "and there is no way I'm doing whatever you brought me here for. Guns or no guns, shit's going down."

"Guys," Bruce stepped between two of the gunmen. "We need him, and I'm sure he will be happy to cooperate. We don't have time to explain the rules, or why they make so much sense. The gardens are dying, and he can help. This is an emergency. I'm Captain Bruce Price, and I've got the authority to take this man in as he is."

The man who had grabbed Rolawndo spoke.

"Hold on," he said.

He thumbed the device clipped to his shoulder, and spoke into it.

"I've got an emergency admission," he said. "Authorized by Captain Bruce Price. His name is…"

The man kept the line open, looked the question at Rolawndo.

Lefty growled, while Rolawndo shrugged.

"Rolawndo Swells," Bruce said.

"Rolawndo Swells," the man repeated into the device, dispassionately.

The noise that came back when he released the button was more static than voice, and Rolawndo couldn't make out a single word in all of it.

Apparently the message was clear enough to the security guards; they all lowered their weapons, and stepped aside.

"Apologies, Captain," the one with the radio nodded. "Proceed."

It was too much to catch all the different combinations that Bruce punched into keypads to get them through the multiple security checkpoints. Rolawndo did notice the level of security increasing as they stepped past one keypad after another. At the last door, the captain was subjected to a thumb print and retina scan after he entered the code. A computer-generated voice asked him to identify himself, and he spoke his name loudly and clearly once more.

There was a soft click, and the door opened. A woman stepped through, and looked them both up and down. Rolawndo raised an eyebrow at her clothes, and her matted and wild hair; an animal hide covered most of her, wrapped awkwardly about her torso to bunch unattractively at her shoulders and fall far past her knees. Her feet were bare, calloused, and stained with layers of what he could only hope was dirt. She stepped toward him, and her smell reached him first; Rolawndo stepped back, took a deep breath, and held it.

"You can't wear those clothes in here," she said. "They won't allow the dog in either."

"No dogs? No clothes?" Rolawndo lifted the other eyebrow.

"You've been waiting for this one," Bruce said. "Rolawndo Swells."

The woman's eyes went wide.

"Oh!" She stepped back. "Come in, I'll bring you right to the garden."

Bruce stepped forward before Rolawndo could, and tried to get a peek around the door frame. He smiled disarmingly at the woman.

"Is it true what they say?" he said. "Are the gardens really-"

"Captain." Her stern voice cut him off as much as her suddenly angling herself between him and the doorway did. She ushered Rolawndo inside, and then Lefty; she pulled the door shut immediately after, calling out as she did.

"Back to your mission, Captain," she cried. "We're back to ours."

Rolawndo turned, and saw what the captain had been trying to catch a glimpse of. Vegetation grew everywhere, in rows that had been deliberately laid out to look natural; it looked sloppy instead, and haphazard. Some of the plants were a lush green; but many had yellowed at the tips of their leaves, and what little fruit that hung from them was shriveled and undersized. He glanced at the woman, to find her looking at him with wide eyes.

"Your garden is in pretty rough shape," he said.

She nodded.

"I know," she said. "That's why you're here. All we know how to do is water, and we can't get enough of it to all the plants."

"Where is your watering schedule?"

Her wide eyes narrowed, and she shook her head.

"We don't have one," she said. "We carry wooden buckets all day, from the spring to the plants, and start over when we reach the end. It takes us about three days to do the whole thing."

"Why don't you irrigate?" Rolawndo frowned. "Where is this spring?"

She pointed.

"At the top of that hill," she said. "There was an irrigation channel, but it washed out. The people who built it weren't here to fix it, and we didn't know how. We blocked the spring in and made a living well out of it instead."

He eyed the hillside, and the withering plants.

"And beyond the hillside?" he said.

"The orchards," she said. "The livestock. And more gardens. Beyond that are the settlements, where all the new Adams and Eves are being raised; but we can't go there."

She looked disdainfully at his jeans and pocket tee.

"Especially wearing that," she added.

Rolawndo took a deep breath, and let it out slowly.

"How many people work the gardens?" he asked.

"Two," she shrugged. "Three, counting you."

"Alright," he said. "We need to start working on trenching out that irrigation system again. We might use part of the pool you made to brew a tea, so start bringing buckets of chickenshit from wherever the chickens are. Is there anywhere specific that bodies are being buried, human or zombie or livestock? We could use a good batch of blood meal."

Her eyes went wide when he said 'chickenshit', but Rolawndo kept talking. When he mentioned dead bodies, and zombies, she went pale.

"There are no…" her voice was a hushed and frightened whisper. "We don't say that word here. We're safe here. This is Eden."

Rolawndo looked around, frowned once more at the yellowing tips and withered fruit.

"The Garden of Eden, huh?" he murmured. "I kind of expected more. And why all the corn? People shouldn't be eating so much corn, you know."

"We inherited the garden," the woman said, her eyes on the sea of imminent decay. "Those that built it were not allowed to be part of the new world, and it was handed over to us. We are the stewards of the Garden of Eden."

"Well, you've done an awful job," Rolawndo said. "If anyone is depending on your skills as gardeners to feed them, they will be hungry soon."

"We know that," she bristled. "It's why we sent for you."

"Alright," he said. "So long as we're clear. We need a notebook or a clipboard, to draw up a watering and work schedule. Where is the other garden worker?"

She was shaking her head, and her hands were suddenly

planted firmly on her hips.

"We can't write anything down here," she snapped. "We shouldn't even be out here, in daylight. The settlers might see us, and have to explain us to the Adams and Eves."

It took a full ten seconds for the breathing exercise that Rolawndo was employing to really kick in. He looked at the woman, full of patience and understanding.

"I'm not ever going to ask about that," he said, at last. "And don't ever mention it to me again. Go get those buckets you were talking about, and start filling them with chickenshit and bringing them back here. I'll be at the spring, seeing about salvaging the irrigation system you folks destroyed."

He didn't wait for her to reply, or walk away. Rolawndo turned on his heel at the last word and walked toward the hillside she had indicated. Lefty barked, and ran on ahead.

Chapter 25

Hefting one guitar in her left hand and the other in her right, she looked appraisingly back and forth between them.

"They are referred to as axes," she noted, aloud.

Leroy gave a little bark.

"Come on, Sarah," Josh said. "You know that isn't why. You can't chop wood with a guitar."

Sarah continued to weigh the guitars, and the possibilities.

"Maybe not wood," she said. "But a howler…maybe."

Josh laughed bitterly.

"Come on, Sarah," he said. "You've seen them."

"There were three of them out there a few days ago," she countered. "Then two ate one, and one ate the other. Now that one is getting weaker, and smaller. I saw that, for sure."

"It's gotten hungrier too," he pointed out.

Sarah set down the heavier one in favor of the sharply cornered one. She hoped it would be sharp enough.

"Okay," she said. "I'm going to go kill that thing, before it gets in here and kills us. You want me to get you anything while I'm out? Beer? Some tacos maybe?"

Josh sighed, and picked up the heavier instrument.

"I still can't believe there are no gardening tools in Harmony Lodge," he said. "We pulled so many out when we set up the studio, I can't believe we didn't miss anything. What I wouldn't give for a nice long scythe right now."

He eyed the guitar again, doubtfully, and approached the door. Sarah had her hand on the heavy crossbar, and was watching him.

"Whenever you're ready," he said.

The bar went flying, and Sarah went flying next. She threw open the door, and burst into the sudden stark daylight. It took a moment for her eyes to adjust, but she kept moving forward. Finally she stopped, and blinked.

It was at her feet, curled up to bake in the sunlight and wait out its prey. The monster leapt to its feet at the sight of her, and howled.

Sarah swung the guitar, her teeth rattling in her head with the sudden jarring impact. The howl was cut short, and the monster fell at her feet again. It swiped at her, but Sarah leapt the talons like a jumprope. When she landed, she brought the guitar down again hard.

It split the skin of the monster's throat, and sent its head to cant at an unnatural angle. She raised it over her shoulder, and the howler leapt to its feet again. Sarah backed up, narrowly escaping another swipe from those talons. The creature lunged, and she backed up another nimble step; then she brought the guitar down on its head, and heard a satisfying squishing sound. She swung again, and again, and stopped.

Her heart pounded in her chest, the guitar was cracked in two places, and the monster's head was a puddle of red and white paste. Sarah wiped her face with the back of her hand, and saw a streak of blood come away. She shrugged, and turned in place. She spoke as she turned, and finished her question even after she had seen her answer.

"Well, that was way more fun than I thought it would be," she said dryly. "Where were you two?"

Josh was on his back, on the ground just outside the door to Harmony Lodge. His arms were locked straight out in front of him, and he was holding the guitar between another howler and his own outstretched arms. Leroy was at the howler's ankle, using the few pounds of leverage and bite he had to tear the monster apart bit by bit. Tiny hunks of mortified flesh had gathered into a pile nearby, and he added two fresh hunks while she watched.

"You're okay, right?" she asked. "I'm going to run and grab my phone, so I get get a picture of this."

Josh's eyes went round, and he shook his head frantically.

"Sarah!" he cried. "A little help!"

She assessed the situation, paused another moment.

"You know that song…" she ventured. "The one you didn't want on the album? The one you said was too-"

"Title track!" Josh shouted. "It's the title track of the next Phantogram album! Come on, Sarah!"

She smiled, and stepped into the swing. It nearly took the monster's head off, and it only took two more quick ones to complete the job. Sarah dropped the guitar on the body. It was nothing but splinters, and a twisted unstrung neck.

Josh took the hand she proffered, and she helped him up. Before either of them could speak, a voice drifted from the woods to them.

"You folks alright?"

They exchanged a glance, and turned to watch several people emerge from the tree line.

"I'm Nick," the same voice called out. It belonged to a tall and wide young man that had a dozen weapons visible on his person. "We were about to take care of them, and come rescue you folks. You kind of beat us to it. Well done. A little crazy, but well done."

Josh raised an eyebrow at Sarah.

"Help was on its way," he said. "All those times I said help was surely on the way, and you kept saying it wasn't. Turns out it was."

Sarah eyed the armed man skeptically.

"Now what?" she asked.

Another voice emerged from the tree line, to the south of where they stood. Nick's hand went to a holstered pistol, seemingly without much thought at all, and Sarah turned to the sound.

"That's what I was wondering too."

A woman emerged from the shadows, dressed in dark leather and holding a sword like she knew how to swing it. A dozen others came into the clearing behind her, armed with more modern weapons. Their automatic rifles made Nick's pistol and blade collection a great deal less threatening.

"Angela Chrysler," the woman said, nodding at Sarah. "This may be totally inappropriate timing, but I love Phantogram. I was really hoping we would find you safe."

She turned her attention to Nick.

"Are you by any chance the good guys?"

Sarah nudged Josh. "She seems like a good egg."

Nick looked back and forth between the women.

"We came here to find them," he said. "And to look for you. The order has made you targets, and we knew we needed to find you first."

"Her?" Angela nodded at Sarah. "Or me?"

"Both of you," Nick said.

"So, Nick," Sarah drawled. "You haven't answered the lady's question. Are you or are you not one of the good guys?"

Nick sighed, relaxed his stance completely and dropped both hands at his sides. He shrugged.

"Honestly," he said, "I don't know. I'm not one of the bad guys, that's for sure. I don't want you folks dead."

Angela glanced at the armed men and women flanking her.

"Is there someone you do want dead?" she ventured.

"Yeah." Nick met her eyes. "The people who will stop at nothing to kill folks like you. I want them dead."

Angela made a motion, and suddenly the rifles all seemed to disappear. She walked forward, sheathing her sword at her side as she approached him. Standing before Nick, she looked up at him and smiled.

"Nice to meet you, Nick." Angela stuck out her hand. "You sound like one of the good guys to me."

He returned her smile, shook her hand and listened as she went on speaking.

"I sure would like a look at that list," she said. "Are Michael and Linda Stern on it? Do you have it with you?"

Nick let go her hand, shook his head.

"I have a short list, the folks I'm going after specifically," he said. "We already found the Sterns, in a lifeboat. They were on a cruise when the outbreak went down, and the ship was sunk. Many people died, but a lot made it too. We have picked up three lifeboats from that liner alone, and they were in one. Last I heard, Mr. Stern was helping Tom Corson-Knowles in the gardens during the day, and they are getting all digital books printed by hand by night."

"You seem pretty proud of yourself," Angela noted.

"I am," Nick nodded. "Not everything I have done these last few weeks has been something to be proud of. The people I have helped to save…the things that they're doing. Yeah, I'm proud of that."

Sarah moved near Angela.

"This list," she said. "What if the people you find aren't on it?"

"We help them too," Nick shrugged. "Of course. We have plenty of food, and we're growing more. Everyone is welcome to join us, or go their own way. It's just that the order is using their list to track them down too, and we are trying to find them all first."

"Or they'll kill us," Sarah finished for him.

Nick nodded.

Angela burst out laughing.

"We've been collecting art," she said, still laughing. "You've been collecting artists!"

She nudged Sarah, and Sarah smiled.

"You've been collecting art," Nick echoed. "That made you a primary target. What the zombies don't destroy of our civilization, the order will."

"Is there somewhere safe from them?" Sarah asked.

Nick nodded. "With room for everyone."

"Can we go there?" Angela said. "All of us, and all the folks back in the city that have been helping?"

He nodded again.

"Can we bring the art?" Angela said.

Nick grinned.

"Yeah," he said. "We can bring the art."

Chapter 26

Allen moved along the end of the rows of vegetables, saw the fruit trees already sprouting near the river bank. He allowed himself a small smile, now that his cheeks were fleshy once more.

A giant tomato plant shifted, and a face peeked out from behind it.

"Allen!"

The woman stood, dusted her pants off and approached him. Her hand was out, and he stepped away instinctively.

"Don't touch me," he hissed, his smile gone.

"It's okay," she said. "The danger has passed, for everyone. I don't think you're contagious any more, even if you can't change back all the way."

He peered at her.

"Do I know you?" Allen cocked his head to the side.

She shook her head, her hand still extended between them.

"I'm a gardener," she said. "And a counselor of sorts. I'm helping folks deal with…the change."

"I do know you." Allen nodded. "You're Christina Hoff Sommers. You wrote-"

"Hush, now," she said, smiling. "That's all gone. I help with the garden now, and with those having trouble adjusting to new food."

Allen glanced at her, sharply, let his eyes drift to the crops.

"I'll never adjust," he said quietly. "Don't waste your time on me."

"I didn't change," Christina said, as if she hadn't heard. "I can't imagine how difficult it must be, even for them. And you…I'm not pretending to understand, Allen. I'm just letting you know I'm here."

They stood there together, for a moment. Her hand was still out, and he finally reached out and took it. Allen felt tears spring to his eyes at the contact, and he blinked them back. Pulling his hand away, he wiped at his eyes with his sleeve.

"I hear you're spending a lot of time in the new pyramid," Christina mused, watching the plants as they drifted with the wind.

Allen nodded.

"They need to be warned," he said.

"Who?" She glanced at him, and back to the plants. "Who needs to be warned? The next generation?"

"No." Allen shook his head. "They'll remember, at least here. It's for fifty generations from now, or a hundred. However long it takes for people to become a danger to themselves again."

"Can I see?" she said.

Their eyes moved at the same time, and met. Allen's brow was furrowed, Christina's face hopeful.

"Do you trust me?" he asked.

"Not to eat me?" Christina laughed. "Yes, Allen. I trust you. We all do. It's why we all let you come and go as you please, like anyone else."

Allen laughed bitterly.

"Not everyone," he retorted. "I hear them talk, even when they aren't talking to me. Plenty do that too, though. They come right up to me, sometimes, and call me zombie or monster or baby eater. Some of them spit in my face, or kick dirt on me."

"I've heard," Christina nodded. "I'm so sorry. No one has set up a way to police or punish folks, but most of us are concerned about protecting you."

"Is that what you are?" he smiled. "My protection?"

She shook her head.

"No," she said. "You're mine. I know you won't act to stop them from treating you with disrespect, but I'm betting you'll stop them from doing it to me. You strike me as a bit of a gentleman, under all that gruff zombie talk."

Allen laughed again.

"Alright," he said. "I'll show you. Maybe you can help me, put the word out about what I still need."

They walked, and watched the crops dwindle from view as the new structure towered above them.

"Have you met Christina McMullen?" Allen asked.

"Briefly," she nodded. "She's a busy lady. I hear she took one look at the pyramids and knew how to rebuild right away. They're even distressing the stones somehow, making it appear to be the same age as the others. That seems strange, to me."

"It would be too confusing, otherwise," Allen said. He picked up his pace, cutting a wide path around workers. They eyed him suspiciously, as a group.

"What do you mean?" Christina frowned, and followed.

"They structures here are more than just housing, or buildings for commerce," Allen said. His voice got lower as they picked their way down a stone passage. "They are messages. The great pyramid is the great message, the key to humanity avoiding extinction. That message was wiped out, when man faced nature. It needs to be remade."

"By you?" Christina asked.

She glanced his way, but neither of them could see the other in the shifting shadows cast by the regularly spaced torches. Her eyes found the path again.

"Only a few people ever saw the message," he said. Allen's voice was barely a whisper. "I'm the only one still alive."

He stopped, and she nearly ran into him.

"Here we are," Allen murmured.

It would have been easy to walk right by it, the way the passage was positioned. Allen felt a chill, the way he always did when he stepped through the doorway. He found the lantern he had been working with, struck a match and slowly illuminated the space.

"Oh!" Christina looked around, turning in place as the light danced across the walls. "You did all this?"

She walked to the depths of the cavern, ran one hand gingerly along the wall. Tracing the lines hewn to show fire, and great groups of people, Christina moved along the wall toward him.

"So few left," she murmured, tracing more lines.

"That's not us," Allen whispered.

Christina stood back at the next set of crude carvings, traced the images of watery death with her eyes as she had traced the others with her fingers.

"Is that the beginning of Christianity?" she asked, leaning in.

Allen laughed. "I'd say having two very important people named 'Christina' around at the beginning might be a good start too."

Her face was hard to read in the shifting shadows.

"Oh, no," she said. "How am I important in all this?"

"You're here," he said. His lantern shifted as he did, and the next stretch of wall was illuminated. "You're going to make sure that signal glows. For thousands of years, maybe tens of thousands."

It was her turn to laugh.

"We're out of batteries," she said. "Officially. Besides, none of the batteries I brought would have done that job."

Allen was immediately very serious, and even he wasn't sure why the sudden sense of urgency gripped him.

"You've got to," he said. "Find someone that can come up with something, some kind of power source that doesn't start to drain until it is activated. That symbol has to glow when this chamber is revealed."

He wouldn't take his eyes off hers, and Allen used every human or zombie power he had within him to convey the seriousness of his request.

"Promise me," he said. "Complete this warning, and see to it that they wall off this section of the pyramid."

His hands were shaking, the one holding the lantern causing the light to dance erratically about the chamber. His brow was wet with sweat, although a fresh chill ran up his spine every few moments.

"You've got to," Allen said again. "You've got to."

He went to the rear of the cave, looked down at a particular spot on the floor, and lowered himself to the sand.

"They won't listen to me," he murmured. "They're all afraid of me. I don't blame them. I'm afraid of me. You have to tell them. You have to do this."

She began to come closer, to speak soothing words that might make him forget that he was a monster for a few more brief moments.

"Go!" Allen shouted. "You can't help me! No one can help me! This is where I belong!"

Christina hesitated.

"I'll never stop dreaming of flesh," he hissed. "I'll never stop wanting to eat people. I'll never be one of you. They're right, I am a monster. I am a zombie. Soon I will be the last zombie, and until I die I will always be a murderer and baby eater. Go, leave me."

He patted the earth next to him, as if the spot had some special significance.

"Leave me here with her," he muttered.

Chapter 27

∞

Each of them carried a large basket laden with fruits and vegetables. They were both smiling, for their own reason. Melissa looked at Rolawndo, as they walked.

"My dad would have liked you," she said.

He nodded, kept walking.

"Underground farming," he said. "I would've liked to have seen that."

"There was so much food in the facility," she said, watching the path. "We were set. We could have lived there indefinitely, and even started to feed and shelter other survivors. When the pulse hit, it was terrifying. Everything shut down. Then the zombies came, and started eating everyone. My dad saved me."

They walked in silence for a minute, before she spoke again.

"You would have liked him too," she pronounced.

He nodded again, continued walking.

A voice cried out behind them, calling their names.

"Melissa!" He sounded distressed. "Rolawndo!"

She turned her head slightly at the sound. Rolawndo showed no sign of having heard. They both kept moving, and carrying the baskets.

"Melissa!" He was getting closer. "Rolawndo!"

She glanced at him, and giggled when she saw how stony Rolawndo's face was. They ignored him, together, and kept walking.

They weren't moving at a furious clip, but they weren't exactly trudging along either. With so many years spent behind a desk, Johns had to choose between calling out and catching up. There was a full minute of blessed silence before the rugged running footfalls came close enough for them to hear. He passed them, visibly huffing and puffing, and planted himself in their path.

"Rolawndo!" he wheezed. "Melissa!"

She veered right, Rolawndo veered left, and they walked around him without breaking stride. As he passed the other man, Rolawndo spoke.

"Warden," he drawled.

Then they were past him, Melissa fighting a giggle while Rolawndo tried not to smile. Another minute of staggered hurried steps, and Johns fell into stride a step behind them. He tried to get between them, but they stayed close. Finally Johns ran around Melissa to look past her at Rolawndo.

"Rolawndo!" he snapped. "Do you know why I'm here?"

He kept walking long enough to let Johns know he was doing a kindness answering him.

"Well," he said, glancing at Melissa, "I guess it isn't to carry food, like the schedule says you should be here for."

"The schedule!" Johns sputtered. "That's the least of your troubles. I need to ask you something, as the new elected peacekeeper in this settlement."

They had arrived at the designated location. The small clearing on the other side of the orchards had become a familiar walk. They never saw who came for the food, but it was always gone when they brought more.

Johns let his proclamation settle while they emptied the baskets carefully on the grass. When it did not get any reaction, he spoke again. With his breath coming back to him at last, Johns sounded himself again.

"Did you hear me?" he said. "I got elected. No more gardening for me. I am the law around here now."

Rolawndo pointed at the man's hip, raised an eyebrow at Melissa.

"Look, Melissa," he said. "The warden graduated from harmless asshole to armed asshole. Some idiot gave this idiot a gun."

Lifting the empty basket, Rolawndo breezed past Johns once more.

"Congratulations," he muttered. "You got the job."

Johns reddened, his hand going to his hip. Neither of them saw, as Melissa had joined Rolawndo in the journey back for more food. Johns reddened further, and called after them.

"I didn't ask for this!" he cried.

"No?" Rolawndo called back. "How did you get it, then? Begging? Blackmailing? Bribing?"

"I was elected!"

Rolawndo didn't reply. As they got further away, Johns raised his voice until he was nearly screaming.

"I could shoot you now!"

Melissa glanced sharply at Rolawndo, and he shook his head slightly.

"You wouldn't!" he called over his shoulder. "All the Adams and Eves would hear, and you would surely answer to someone."

They had another minute of blessed silence before he caught up again, and Rolawndo found himself wondering if it would be the last of their quiet comfortable moments together. He caught her eye as the pounding footfalls came closer, and gave her a small smile.

"Hold on, now," Johns said, falling into step beside Rolawndo.

They didn't hold on, or break stride. Johns was perspiring heavily. It took another full minute for him to catch his breath enough to speak. When he did, it came out in broken groupings of words that were not quite sentences.

"I have reason…" he gasped, "…to believe…that you…are making bourbon."

Melissa was clearly torn between being shocked and breaking out into a fresh giggle fit. Rolawndo kept his eyes on the path, and frowned. After it became clear that he was not going to comment, Johns wheezed out a few more batches of words.

"Do you deny…" he puffed, "…this accusation… Rolawndo Swells?"

Rolawndo looked at Melissa, turning his attention from him.

"Did that sound like an accusation?" he asked her.

She shrugged, visibly struggling to contain her laughter.

"Are you making bourbon?" she giggled.

Rolawndo shrugged.

"Maybe," he said. "If the still works. We'll know tonight."

"I knew it!" Johns ran in front of them, blocked Rolawndo's path.

"Hang on," he said. "You're coming with me."

Rolawndo tried to walk past as he had before, and Johns grabbed his arm roughly about the bicep.

"Take your hand off me," Rolawndo muttered.

"You're coming with me," Johns repeated. He didn't go anywhere, however; and his grip on Rolawndo's arm loosened uncertainly.

Turning his head slowly, Rolawndo made sure the other man saw the seriousness within him when he spoke again.

"Take your fucking hand off me," he said quietly. "Or try to get to that gun before I do. Either way, decide now."

Johns let him go, and stepped back.

"This is unacceptable," he said. His hand went slowly to his hip as he continued to back away, and Melissa called out as she stepped between them.

"No!" she cried.

The sound of her voice was lost in a loud whooping siren. The sudden noise was so startling, Rolawndo dove for her. They went down in a heap at Johns' feet, as he fumbled the pistol loose at last. It tumbled from his hand to land inches from where Rolawndo's hand was planted. He picked up the gun with distaste, and stood slowly. Reaching out, he took Melissa's hand. The warbling siren sound continued to fill the valley while he helped her to her feet.

"What is that?" he cried.

"An attack!" Johns said. "It's an attack. Give me back my gun!"

Rolawndo clicked the chamber open, tilted the pistol and spun the cylinder slowly. One by one, the rounds dropped into his open palm. When it was empty, he tossed the bullets over his shoulder. The gun he threw as far into the tree line as he could. Johns dashed after it, and he turned to Melissa.

"I'm getting my dog," he said. "And I'm getting out of here."

She watched Johns stumbling over open ground to disappear behind the first stand of trees. Melissa turned to Rolawndo, reached out and grasped his hand.

"Take me with you," she said. "Please."

Chapter 28

The body beside her was inhuman, as were the sounds that escaped between its parted and pointed teeth. Michelle moved closer in her sleep, and the creature shifted to press itself against her. It lay there silent for another minute, then lifted its head. It barked.

Michelle stirred sleepily.

"Mammoth," she murmured. "Hush, buddy. It's just the waves."

He barked again.

"Or the seagulls," she muttered. "Go back to sleep."

She patted the cot beside her, closed her eyes.

Mammoth got up, moved to the doorway.

She moaned, and rolled over.

"Really?" Michelle sat up, rubbed the sleep from her eyes. "You need to go now?"

It had been a real effort to train him to relieve himself on deck. For their first few days at sea, he had grown increasingly uncomfortable. When he began to refuse food, she had suddenly realized why. After many unsuccessful attempts, Michelle had finally coaxed him into resuming his natural cycle. Of all the details she might share about how she had survived the apocalypse, if she survived the apocalypse, the things she did to coax a dog to take a dump on deck would remain between her and him forever.

Michelle opened the door, backed up and let it swing

inward. The moment it was clear, Mammoth darted out on deck and started barking. She hadn't heard him bark like that in awhile, and Michelle wrapped a blanket around herself instinctively before trailing him.

A boat had pulled up alongside her vessel, dwarfing her last little bit of drifting luck. Michelle saw people leaning against the railing, waving down at her. For a long moment she stared, as if in a dream. Then a shudder passed through her body, and Michelle began waving at the unfamiliar faces with both hands. Her motions were a little wild, and the blanket unwound itself to drift to the deck; but she didn't care. Michelle had stopped counting her days at sea many days ago; none of them had featured faces other than hers or her furry companion's.

"Oy!" Michelle called out, still waving her arms. "Hello!"

The people on deck were also waving, looking like a bedraggled but overall friendly bunch. They parted from one section of the railing, and a woman stepped to it. She put a hand on the railing, the other in the air, and called out.

"Ahoy!" she cried. "Is everyone on board okay? Do you need food or water?"

Michelle stepped forward, dropped her hands.

"It's just me," she called out, "and him. We're fine. Just out of gas and scared and maybe a little lonely."

The woman grinned, and it nearly brought tears to Michelle's eyes. She blinked them away as she let her eyes drift to the side of the other craft. Someone had clearly painted over whatever the vessel's name had been, and painted a new name by hand over the cover up.

"The H.M.S. Slush Brain?" she asked, glancing at Mammoth. She hadn't meant for the other woman to hear across the water, but many days speaking only to herself and him had perhaps affected her volume modulation.

Michelle watched the woman nod, and grin again.

"That's right!" she called out. "You have found the H.M.S. Slush Brain, or we have found you. I am Angela Chrysler, captain of this vessel. It is my pleasure to officially welcome you aboard."

Michelle's head spun with questions as a rope ladder was lowered from one deck to the other.

"Her Majesty's Service?" she asked. "Slush Brain? Angela Chrysler? I know that name."

Angela laughed, and Michelle felt her eyes fill with tears again at the carefree sound.

"No matter," she said. "No need for explanations now; and it's a bit of an inside joke, besides. Come on, climb aboard."

Michelle knelt beside Mammoth, stroked his fur.

"He's coming too," she said. "He should go up first."

Michelle relaxed when she saw Angela nodding. One of the men leaning over the deck shook his head.

"He's gigantic," he said. "How do we get him up here?"

"I've got a long board down here," Michelle said. "If someone could help me get one end of it up there…"

She trailed off, as Angela nodded again. Two men clambered down the ladder, both of them smiling at her in passing. It was all she could do not to burst into tears, and she knelt beside Mammoth with her face in his fur until the feeling passed.

"We're being rescued, boy," she murmured.

They were on the higher deck a few minutes later, and Mammoth was making new friends fast. Michelle held back, watching, until the captain approached and took her in her arms. Angela held her, and Michelle embraced her back. She kept the tears at bay, but she soaked in the caring contact like it was food. Michelle stepped back after a minute, smiled at last.

"Thank you," she said.

"Absolutely," Angela nodded. "Do you need anything from your boat?"

"No." Michelle frowned again. "I know I'm in my pajamas and socks, but they're the cleanest clothes I've got. Everything else…"

She drifted off, and Angela spoke when she didn't pick it up again.

"From another life, hmmm?" She smiled. "Come on. Let's get you some fresh clothes."

Michelle forgot herself for a moment as they passed through the people on deck. She grabbed Angela's elbow, and gasped. It was a startling transformation, as the other woman brushed Michelle back and drew a sword from her hip in one fluid motion. Michelle stumbled, and staggered backwards to plop her butt hard on the deck. Mammoth barked, and Angela collected herself in as little time as it had taken for the first transformation to take place.

Angela sheathed the sword.

"Sorry," she said. "Post-apocalyptic jitters."

She extended a hand to Michelle, and helped her up.

"I was just going to say…" Michelle said, glancing back at the passengers they had passed. "I think I recognize some of your passengers. Was that Doug Benson back there, the American comic? And Megan O'Russell, the actress?"

"Yep." Angela nodded. "Ask Doug about how he saved the world sometime. It takes a little coaxing, and he's super humble in the way he tells it; but it's an amazing story, and he makes it hilarious somehow. He's not the only comic we have on board either. Ari Shaffir is around here somewhere."

"What kind of boat is this?" Melissa asked. "What boat has a bunch of famous passengers, at a time like this?"

Angela laughed again, and continued to lead the way.

"Wait till you meet my crew," she said over her shoulder.

Chapter 29

Watching the monsters feed, Rolawndo knelt in the dense underbrush and petted Lefty calmly. He waved Melissa down every time she made as if to move to his side. Holding a finger to his lips, he hushed them both in his mind. The howlers continued to feed, ignoring the guns that had fallen at their feet. When they had consumed the last of the flesh that had clung to the outposts' bones a minute before, they moved swiftly toward the mountain Rolawndo had just finished crossing. He watched them until they were gone, counted silently to ten, and motioned to Melissa.

She rose from her crouch, as he stepped onto the path. He hadn't taken three steps before a series of clicks and clacks sounded from the bushes opposite where they had been hiding.

"Come on out," he called softly.

A man stood, aiming a pistol Rolawndo's way.

"Hold it right there," he said. "All of you."

Rolawndo shook his head.

"You shoot us," he said, "and those things will come back."

"I don't want to shoot you," the man said. "We need your help. I've come to bring you back. We're prepared to make you another offer. Folks like you are needed elsewhere as well."

"On your sinking island?" Rolawndo frowned. "Where you are rewriting history? No, thanks. Let us go."

"Rolawndo…" Melissa murmured.

He reached back, took her hand. It may have looked like a simple reassurance to the casual onlooker; but he had never touched her like that, and she fell suddenly silent. Gripping his hand, she watched the creature emerge from the trees behind the armed man. Rolawndo felt her holding her breath, and realized that he was holding his too.

Rolawndo breathed, and smiled. "Your move, man."

The man lifted the pistol to eye level, his face hitting the dirt hard the next moment.

"Go!" Rolawndo pushed Melissa down the path, pointed resolutely and shouted at Lefty.

"Go!"

The man was already missing an arm, and had paled by several shades. As a member of the order, he had been inoculated when commanded to do so. Rather than turn to a monster that may one day become a man again, he succumbed to death as Rolawndo dove to the ground beside him. He rose, gripping the pistol in both hands, and shot the creature twice in the chest. It rolled back, and leapt to its feet. The next bullet glanced off its skull, and the next buried itself deep in the monster's left eye. It went down, and he kept the sites trained on it as it fell.

It didn't stir for one second, then two, then three. Rolawndo felt no need to toe the corpse, to make sure it was indeed a corpse; he stuffed the pistol in his waistband and ran down the path at full speed.

Before long he came to the sea, and Melissa.

"Where's Lefty?" he asked.

She pointed, and grinned. A cluster of trees was rooted at the water's edge, their branches dangling a dense wall of leaves. Through the scant random openings in the greenery, he saw floating stark blue and white.

"On the boat," Michelle said.

They moved across the bank, and took control of the little craft.

Rolawndo pressed a button, smiling at the forgotten sound of an engine firing up. He unwound the rope that was holding it hidden in overhanging foliage, and engaged the throttle.

A voice called out from the shore, and they turned to look at the same time.

"Is that Johns?" she asked.

"Uh huh."

Melissa frowned. "What's he saying?"

Rolawndo turned to look ahead again.

She turned too.

"I don't know," he smiled.

Shots rang out, and he pulled her and Lefty to the floor.

"I should have killed that son of a bitch when I had the chance," he muttered.

"Do you mean that?"

Melissa was looking up at him, slightly lower than him on the floor of the boat. He shrugged.

"This wouldn't be happening," he pointed out.

The shots stopped, and Rolawndo wondered if he was reloading. There was no need to get up too fast; they were headed in the right direction, away from the island at last. After a full minute had passed, he raised his head. Melissa started to follow suit, but he waved her down again. Once more, he watched someone get eaten by a monster. This time, he was not nearly as dismayed by the sight.

When the body was gone, and they had drifted too far for details, he motioned for her to stand up. Melissa rose slowly, staring ahead of them intently. He thought she was resisting the urge to look back, until she spoke softly.

"Do you see that?" she said. "That's the ship that brought me in, or one just like it."

Rolawndo peered into the fading light, and nodded.

"Yeah," he said. "Me too."

"What do you think they're doing?" she asked.

"Probably heading out again." He glanced at her. "To rescue more people."

"Rescue?" She turned to him. "Or enslave?"

He shrugged. "You say tomato…"

She didn't smile, even when he nudged her.

"There's something else in the water," she said.

Melissa moved to the edge of the boat, looked over the side.

She screamed.

Backing into Rolawndo, trembling, she tilted the boat precariously.

"Whoa, have a seat." Rolawndo pulled her down beside him, let her bury her head in his shoulder. While she shook with sobs, he peered cautiously over the side of the little craft.

There were dozens of bodies floating all around them, bleeding out into the ocean and missing the part of them that was there to move them around. The heads floated nearby, eyes closed or staring into the forever of the sky above or the sea below.

Rolawndo shuddered, and held her closer.

Chapter 30

Lauren raced across the desert, following the footprints in the drifting sand. Her heart pounding, she ran faster when she glimpsed a form far ahead of her. It was blurred, and moving quickly; she tilted forward, and sprinted over the sand.

He was almost to the docks.

"Nick!" she cried, or tried to; it came out a wheeze, and slowed her pace. Lauren swallowed the urge to call out again, and kept running.

He was making ready to cast off when she reached the shore.

"Nick!"

She came to a halt, panting and resting her hands on her knees.

"What are you doing?" she asked.

He stood up straight, turned to her.

"I'm going to stop him," he said.

Lauren's face twisted in confusion.

"Stop who?" she said. "You don't mean…Nick, did you go through my things?"

"I did the same thing you did," he shrugged. "I found myself questioning my leaders, and decided I should know what they know. I saw that there's only one ship left, besides yours. He's killing people, and I am going to stop him."

Lauren stood, started moving across the beach toward

him. Nick cast off, and drifted away faster than she could follow.

"Nick!" she cried. "Come back! You can't do this alone! He's a heartless killer!"

"I'm a killer too, Lauren," he called back. "And I seem to have lost my heart somewhere along the way. It seems only fitting that I should be the one to go after him."

"There's an override code!" she shouted. "For the boat!"

"I know!" he called back. "I finally know everything! Or at least enough to make a difference!"

He turned his back, and she watched the forward lamp spear across the water as the sun dipped low over the horizon. Lauren dropped to her knees again, and watched the light until it had disappeared.

On board, Nick kept his thoughts clear and his mind focused. He remembered his training, and ran through scenarios in his head as he closed in on the other vessel. As soon as he saw the other ship's lights, he extinguished his own. He saw another small boat in the distance, and let himself be curious for the space of a full second. Then he turned to his task, and prepared for his mission.

It was less organized on board than he had planned for. The guards were all men, and drunk, and easy to kill quietly. The way they were spaced throughout the ship, Nick found himself wondering if anyone on board had any military experience at all. He only killed the ones he came across, twisting their heads until he heard a satisfying snap or sinking his knife deep into their hearts until they were still. By the time he approached the captain's cabin, he was covered in blood and his eyes were jittering wildly in their sockets.

Nick punched in the override code, and opened the door.

Three shots rang out, and they all found their way up

an empty passageway to thunk harmlessly against a steel door. Three more followed, for no apparent reason; then a smoking muzzle poked through the door. Nick shook his head, a little disappointed, and grabbed it. The hand holding it wouldn't let go, so he twisted until it did.

Reversing the gun, Nick emptied the clip into the man. His face exploded, then his chest, and he fell to the floor.

Nick strode across the cabin, knocked the gun from the captain's hand and lifted him by his neck. His eyes were pounding now, too big for his head, and he felt muscle and tendon shift under his fingers.

He squeezed, and felt his blood pumping. He squeezed harder, and watched the captain's mouth fall open. Bruce reached out, to pull his arms away; but the steel rage that flowed through Nick was clamped about his throat, and his strength was that of a child.

Nick squeezed, used every ounce of strength that the rage was feeding him, felt the skin start to give way under his fingers. The captain tried to emit a strangled cry, but only a tortured wheeze came out.

A noise like he had never thought he could make escaped Nick's lips, and the animal sound brought with it another wave of animal strength. His fingers dug into the other man's throat, and blood burst in his face. Nick turned his head to the side, wrapped his fingers tight around the man's larynx, and pulled. The body fell to the floor, a fountain of blood spraying from what had once been the man's throat, and Nick dropped the bloody hunk of flesh next to his dead staring eyes.

Turning, blood dripping from his fingers, Nick saw the forms shadowing the doorway.

He chuckled; the sound was low, dark, and humorless.

"He's dead," he said. "Your mission has been aborted."

"I disagree," one drawled. "I see here that someone

punched in an override code. I figure that was likely you. So, I have a deal for you. You punch in that code on the main control board, and sign me in as captain, and I'll let you live. Or we'll kill you, take a few lifeboats, and go raid that settlement you came from. Hell, the way I see it you did us a favor. We were about to do old Bruce in, and get on with hunting down the privileged."

Nick looked at the man, at the others nodding behind him.

"Bruce was hunting the capable," he said. "To let humanity have a better chance, even if it was a twisted and misguided one."

"He talks like the captain," one of the men said, glancing at the one who had spoken earlier. "Can't we just kill him?"

Nick sighed.

"I'll give you the code," he said. "It doesn't matter. Everything is lost. Go to the pyramids. Blow up the settlement. Kill everyone. I don't care."

The aspiring captain nudged the other man.

"See?" he jeered. "Killing is not always the answer. Almost always, but not quite."

He put a pistol as close to Nick's head as he could get it without making it easy to swipe away. Nick nodded, impressed at last.

"Punch in the code," the man sneered.

Nick nodded once more, and moved to the cabin control panel.

"It's easy," he said. "You just key the code, and select the option you want."

His fingers moved as he spoke, and had moved through three pages before he fully explained what he had done.

"See?" he said lightly. "The order is very literal. Just type the word 'override', select 'self-destruct vessel', tap 'in ten seconds' and then tap 'enter'.

The man's eyes went wide as he moved to view the screen, and Nick's dark laughter began behind him.

"No more killing," Nick said, still laughing. "In five... four...three..."

The man shot him, in the face and the chest. Nick fell to the floorboards.

Then the ship exploded.

From a mile away, across the open water, Melissa and Rolawndo watched. She grasped his hand when the vessel turned to a floating fireball, and watched the endless flaming pieces of boat and bodies rain into the sea a few moments later. Some continued to burn, others were snuffed out as they touched the ocean; none of them were big enough to be a survivor, even if every piece hadn't been scorched.

Rolawndo turned the rudder, slightly.

"What are you doing?" Melissa asked.

"That was the ship I came in on," he said. "The one that dumped those bodies, the bodies of those that refused to be intellectually enslaved. We saw the boat approaching it, and we saw which direction it came from. Whoever was on that boat just killed Captain Bruce, and his mindless cronies. We're going to meet that person's friends."

Chapter 31

$$\infty$$

It seemed only natural that the table should be a round one, and large enough to seat a number of people. Nonetheless, all eyes were on one woman. Christina scanned the table, and nodded.

"Please make sure everyone learns what you learn here tonight. There is good news, and bad news, and everyone needs to know the truth of the matter either way."

"Too bad you weren't in charge before," a voice called out. "With the easy access of the internet, you could have formed a completely transparent government that could let everyone know what was going on immediately. We could have voted online, and made decisions together, and done away with all misrepresentative representation."

Christina smiled, and nodded.

"Thank you, Rolawndo," she said. "We're doing the best we can, and I'm glad you approve."

"And you have bourbon," he nodded, raising his glass. "Like a polite society should."

She laughed, and spread her hands.

"May I go on?"

"Of course," he said. "Please."

"Adam Dreece put together a team that was able to tap into a satellite unaffected by the pulse," she said.

Christina waved her hand Adam's way, and he nodded.

"We were," he said. "What we saw was both relieving

and disconcerting. The cities are gone, turned to rubble by zombies and rats and seemingly accelerated natural growth. It would be harder to start over in any area that was once a city than it would be in the middle of nowhere. We really are in the best place we can be, from the looks of things."

"Eden was being invaded," Rolawndo said. "When we left, howlers were attacking the perimeter."

"They never got in," Adam answered. "The island looks the same as Christina's. The perimeter is bristling with heavy firepower; the inner area is completely free of weapons. The similarities end there, however; one island is full of people working on non-violent technology, and the other island is apparently deliberately eschewing all technology."

"At least it isn't sinking," Christina murmured.

"It may as well be," Rolawndo put in. "They won't let anyone write anything down, or talk about the past, or plan for the future. It may not be sinking, but it isn't going anywhere."

"Any place the order is in charge is deliberately doomed."

Lauren had been quiet since Nick had disappeared, though she still attended all meetings and discharged all her duties in a way that left nothing to be desired. At the sound of her voice, every head at the table turned.

"That's why you're all here," she muttered. "You need to save humanity. Not controlled humanity, not programmed humanity, not some version of humanity that hungers to be told what to do."

She fell silent, and looked down at her hands on the table. Rolawndo leaned forward, a couple seats down, and slid a glass across the table to her. Lauren looked at it, laughed bitterly, and drank the entire contents in one long draught. She coughed, set the glass down, and rose from the table. After she had crossed the room, and walked out the door, Allen stood as well. Wordlessly, he crossed the room and exited quietly.

"There is good news," Adam said.

The room's attention went from the empty exit to him, and he went on.

"There are no more zombies, as far as we can tell." Adam smiled. "They have all died, or turned back to humans. We are alone on the Earth again, and we can find the remaining survivors with ease now."

Most of the people interested in attending the meeting were able to find a seat at the table. Seats were lined along the walls, for anyone else that wanted to sit in, and more of them filled up with every meeting. Most of the onlookers didn't speak, although they were free to. Tonight one did.

"What about that one?" he called out. "The one that just left. He's still zombie, isn't he? I heard he can't change back."

Adam nodded.

"Allen is in a unique position indeed," he said. "First of all, he may be the only person at this settlement that can say that he is in some way responsible for each of us still being alive. Many of us he saved more than once. He is also unfortunately unable to turn back completely; but with the amount of medication we have on hand he will always be almost completely human."

"Unless he eats someone," another voice called out.

"We are not the order," Christina said firmly, "but we will not tolerate violence any more than they will. We will not, however, peek into people's lives or shackle them for what they might do. We will all together decide what we must do, when anyone raises a hand against another."

It was not unusual or unexpected to see two men get up and walk out, as Christina spoke again; everyone was free to come and go as they pleased. She deferred to another, and nodded his way.

"Harv Eker has been hard at work with his own team. Harv," she said. "You have been building an educational center. Would you please tell these folks about it?"

Chapter 32

∞

Allen studied his face carefully in the mirror. Transforming so many times over such a short period had taken its toll on him. He looked older than he had before, and there were lines on his face where the skin had once looked smooth and youthful. Still he looked, and met his own gaze in the mirror. That was where the real change had taken place; not in the new lines around his eyes, but in their dark depths.

Those eyes had burned rusted red, and seen heat signatures fleeing from him in abject terror. They had changed from human to monster and back again so many times Allen couldn't count. In all the changing, a new depth had been recklessly plumbed in Allen's soul. The terrors of the world and the stark savagery of his own hunger had raked out deeper layers of darkness within him, and it showed in his eyes.

He held his own gaze, thinking of what he had been spending his days and nights on, remembering the slow calm acceptance that one person after another had begun to show him. Allen felt the loving arms of the community slowly encircling him, and felt himself relaxing into its sweet embrace more every day. Soon the carvings would be complete, and he would put his usefulness to work wherever it might be needed.

Smiling at his own reflection, grateful for the string

of second chances that had led him to smiling at his own reflection, Allen took a single pill from the bottle on the counter. He swallowed it, dry. Turning from the mirror, he pulled on a light jacket and stepped into the cool night air.

The path to the pyramid brought him past the meeting hall once more, and Allen smiled again as he stopped outside. There were good people in there, and good things being made; and somehow they welcomed him as one of them. He knew he could walk back through that door, take a seat and have a voice; he knew that everyone here felt the same way. His smile broadened to a grin as he stood there, and he didn't hear the footfalls in the sand behind him at all.

A sudden flaring pain exploded in the back of his head, and Allen's mouth was suddenly full of sand. After a moment he realized that he was lying facedown in the desert, and had been struck from behind; Allen rolled over, shielding his face with his hands.

The club separated his fingers, and drove them into his own face. A moment of bursting light behind his eyes was followed by the bitter taste of his own blood in his mouth. Allen had time to wonder if his nose or his fingers were broken, or if it was both, before the next blow landed.

He spit out a mouthful of teeth and blood, and fended off the next blow with his forearm. Allen let the rage rise in him, as he got his feet under him. He opened his mouth, to howl his hunger, and lunged at the man.

Three shots rang out from behind him. The first found his spine, and Allen's legs went ragged mid-flight; the second split the skin of his neck down one side, and opened a fountain of blood that spurted to the sand below. The third shot found the back of his skull, and Allen's face exploded to become an ugly and unrecognizable exit wound. His body hit the sand at the man's feet, to twitch and bleed silently.

The door to the meeting hall swung inward, and a half dozen lights speared into the night. They settled on the faces of the two men: one standing over Allen's disfigured corpse, the other with an actual smoking gun in his hand. The shooter tossed the weapon in the sand, and dove on the body. He sawed at the remains of Allen's neck until someone stepped forward to stop him; as he was pulled off the body, the head rolled in the sand.

"Guilty as charged," the man said, dropping the knife and holding up his bloody hands.

The other did the same, putting his hands up and getting on his knees.

"Me too," he said. "Guilty as charged. Go ahead. Execute us."

"Hold on."

Michael Stern stepped forward, spread his hands.

"No one said anything about execution," he said calmly. "Can anyone speak for these two men?"

"I've seen them," Melissa nodded, moved close enough to Rolawndo to nudge him. "Remember? They were security in Eden."

Rolawndo nodded.

"Yeah," he said. "They're members of the order. Let's send them back."

The men both paled visibly, and the man that had been standing fell to his knees beside the other.

"No," he shook his head. "This is the way it has to be."

Christina shook her head.

"I think we've all had enough killing," she muttered.

There was a general murmur of assent.

"We're problem solvers," Stern nodded. "Not executioners."

Another wave of positive voices rose, and then a thin peal of laughter cut through it. Lauren stepped from the shadows, and strode across the sand to look down at the men.

"Don't you see?" she laughed. "You are the savages, you are the ones who ruin everything by making it happen the same way every time. These people are humanity's hope; you are its enemy."

She dropped to her knees, stared them each in the eye in turn.

"I would have killed you," she sneered. "I would have shot you in the face until you didn't have faces to shoot at anymore. I would have done it without compunction, without hesitation and without remorse. That's what the order made me, that's what your rules turned me into, that's who I nearly ended up being in the end. We will bind you in your boat, and send it back to Eden. When you get there, you will wish we had taken your monstrous faces as I would like to."

She stood, and walked up to Christina.

"With your permission," she said, "I will send word to the order that their final mission has been thwarted."

"It doesn't matter," the shooter spat, waving his bloody hands. "The last zombie is dead. That was our mission."

Lauren kept her back to him, aiming her response at the group.

"That was half of their mission," she said. "The other half was to turn us into executioners. You made a different decision than that, without any word from me that you should. The order needs to know that. They need to know that you are doing things differently. They need to see that you are the ones that are making your decisions."

Christina lifted an eyebrow.

"Lauren?" she said. "Are you going somewhere?"

She nodded.

"I'll take them back," Lauren said. "I'm as much an

outsider here as Allen was, maybe more. I belong with savage people like me."

"They'll kill you." The shooter stood, and sneered at her back.

Lauren turned, smiled.

"Maybe," she said. "Maybe not. Either way, I get to see their faces when they see yours. That's worth it. Although I suspect that with Rolawndo escaping you folks need all the garden knowledge you can get. I'm more likely to become a member in high standing among the gardeners or security, with my background. Either way, I'll be sure to spread your shameful story. Two monsters creeping up on a man to kill him. Because they were told to."

"He was the monster," he shooter frowned.

"He," Lauren said, her eyes on the body, "was more a man than you'll ever be."

Epilogue

Quite some time later…

The cavern was open, and inviting, difficult as it had been to find. Their lanterns cast light deep into the opening, and shadows beyond.

"Should we go find the professor?"

Her voice echoed off the walls, and he smiled in response.

"Not just yet," he said. "Let's have a look."

He brought his lantern close to one wall, as she drifted further into the darkened space. They called to each other, at the same time.

"Mara!" he cried softly.

"Alan!" she said, in a fierce whisper.

They both laughed, and he waved his lantern at the wall.

"Take a look at these carvings," he said. "There's something strange about them…they seem familiar, although I can't remember ever seeing anything like them before. Come here, have a look."

"Alan," she said again.

Her voice was deeper, and lower, and it made him turn. Alan held his lamp toward her, saw nothing but shifting shadows beyond the dancing light.

"I think we should find the professor," Alan said. His voice trembled a little, and he didn't know why. He noticed a strange symbol on the wall, pulsing with an unnatural illumination. Leaning in closer, he narrowed his eyes.

"Mara," he said, a little uneasily. "This thing is glowing. That's not possible. I think we need to find the professor."

Her voice came from the shadows again; Alan felt his heart go out to her in response, as it always did.

"Alan," she said. "Come here."

He lowered his lamp, turned her way, followed the sound of her voice.

"I have something I want to show you."

Dear Reader,

Thank you for taking this journey with me. Writing these books turned my stomach, twisted my heart and stirred my soul. The number of tears I cried writing and editing this story were beyond counting; and when it touched me so deeply, I knew I could be proud in sharing it. I hope it touched you too, and that you are as glad for having read it as I am for having written it.

You may see authors as I used to, busy folks who don't much care how their books affect their readers. We're busy folks, most of us; but knowing that people love our books actually often means a great deal to us. The author shares in a way that no other artist does, and we are aware that it is our own stark self that shows in everything we write. No matter how many times we have heard from someone who loves our books, the experience never stops being a sacred and special one.

I suggested that you subscribe to my newsletter, The Secret Society of Deeper Meaning, in the foreword. Now that you've gotten to know me a bit better, you might feel more compelled to join up. If you're already a member… well, then you already know how I feel about you. I won't get all sappy on you here; wait for your monthly email.

If you don't want to belong to a secret society, even if it is my favorite secret society ever, that's okay. There are other ways to reach out. One is to leave a review. It will not just be read by me; it will also be read by other readers looking for a new book to read. Leaving a review helps readers find the authors they will love, and I for one am grateful every time someone leaves a review for one of my books.

Or, just shoot me a message. Telling me that I made you cry will assuredly make me cry, and simply saying 'thanks for writing' touches me pretty deeply as well. I'm a busy guy, so be patient…but I will get back to you. I feel blessed to have this opportunity, and even more blessed to see how this opportunity can connect me with others. When the bridge between us is my books, I see that as a special connection indeed. If you don't feel like reaching out electronically, just take a moment. Say 'thanks, Jay' under your breath or in your mind; I like to think that that energy can ride the network of energy that is everything and find its way to me somehow. Either way, know you made a friend in that moment.

That might be too much for some folks, and that's okay too. You did the thing I wanted you to do most; you read this book. That's a special thing, and I hope you detect the sincerity in my gratitude when I thank you for it. Until next time…

Thanks for reading!

All the best,
Jay
Jay@JayNorry.com
Twitter: @JayNorry
The Secret Society of Deeper Meaning
Founding Member

P.S. See, I am an insufferable goofball. Please take me very seriously.

Also available from J.K. Norry. . .

Dreaming The Perpetual Dream

<u>The Ringer</u>
Ringing in a Voyage
Ringing in a New Year

<u>Zombie Zero</u>
Zombie Zero: The First Zombie
Zombie Zero: The Last Zombie

<u>Zombie Zero: The Short Stories</u>
Volume 1: The Sickness Spreads
Volume 2: The Beginning of the End
Volume 3: Love Lost at Sea
Volume 4: The Zombie Killers
Volume 5: Monstrous Consequences
Volume 6: The Heart of the Monster

<u>Walking Between Worlds</u>
Demons & Angels (Book I)
Rise of the Walker King (Book II)
Fall of the Walker King (Book III)
The Demon Be Damned

<u>As Jay Norry</u>
Words Are Made Up!
Earth Is In Space!
Stumbling Backasswards Into the Light

Learn more about the author at **www.JayNorry.com**

www.ingramcontent.com/pod-product-compliance
Lightning Source LLC
Chambersburg PA
CBHW030026200726
48283CB00012B/1062